D0195194

The Thought Readers

Mind Dimensions: Book 1

Dima Zales

♠ Mozaika Publications ♠

Published by Mozaika Publications, an imprint of Mozaika LLC.
www.mozaikallc.com

Cover by Najla Qamber Designs
www.najlaqamberdesigns.com

Edited by Adian Editing and Mella Baxter

e-ISBN: 978-1-63142-021-4
Print ISBN: 978-1-63142-027-6

DESCRIPTION

Everyone thinks I'm a genius.

Everyone is wrong.

Sure, I finished Harvard at eighteen and now make crazy money at a hedge fund. But that's not because I'm unusually smart or hardworking.

It's because I cheat.

You see, I have a unique ability. I can go outside time into my own personal version of reality—the place I call "the Quiet"—where I can explore my surroundings while the rest of the world stands still.

I thought I was the only one who could do this—until I met *her*.

My name is Darren, and this is how I learned that I'm a Reader.

.

CHAPTER ONE

Sometimes I think I'm crazy. I'm sitting at a casino table in Atlantic City, and everyone around me is motionless. I call this the *Quiet*, as though giving it a name makes it seem more real—as though giving it a name changes the fact that all the players around me are frozen like statues, and I'm walking among them, looking at the cards they've been dealt.

The problem with the theory of my being crazy is that when I 'unfreeze' the world, as I just have, the cards the players turn over are the same ones I just saw in the Quiet. If I were crazy, wouldn't these cards be different? Unless I'm so far gone that I'm imagining the cards on the table, too.

But then I also win. If that's a delusion—if the pile of chips on my side of the table is a delusion—then I might as well question everything. Maybe my name isn't even Darren.

No. I can't think that way. If I'm really that confused, I don't want to snap out of it—because if I do, I'll probably wake up in a mental hospital.

Besides, I love my life, crazy and all.

My shrink thinks the Quiet is an inventive way I describe the 'inner workings of my genius.' Now that sounds crazy to me. She also might want me, but that's beside the point. Suffice it to say, she's as far as it gets from my datable age range, which is currently right around twenty-four. Still young, still hot, but done with school and pretty much beyond the clubbing phase. I hate clubbing, almost as much as I hated studying. In any case, my shrink's explanation doesn't work, as it doesn't account for the way I know things even a genius wouldn't know—like the exact value and suit of the other players' cards.

I watch as the dealer begins a new round. Besides me, there are three players at the table: Grandma, the Cowboy, and the Professional, as I call them. I feel that now-almost-imperceptible fear that accompanies the phasing. That's what I call the process: phasing into the Quiet. Worrying about my sanity has always facilitated phasing; fear seems helpful in this process.

I phase in, and everything gets quiet. Hence the name for this state.

It's eerie to me, even now. Outside the Quiet, this casino is very loud: drunk people talking, slot machines, ringing of wins, music—the only place louder is a club or a concert. And yet, right at this moment, I could probably hear a pin drop. It's like I've gone deaf to the chaos that surrounds me.

Having so many frozen people around adds to the strangeness of it all. Here is a waitress stopped mid-step, carrying a tray with drinks. There is a woman about to pull a slot machine lever. At my own table, the dealer's hand is raised, the last card he dealt hanging unnaturally in midair. I walk up to him from the side of the table and reach for it. It's a king, meant for the Professional. Once I let the card go, it falls on the table rather than continuing to float as before—but I know full well that it will be back in the air, in the exact position it was when I grabbed it, when I phase out.

The Professional looks like someone who makes money playing poker, or at least the way I always imagined someone like that might look. Scruffy, shades on, a little sketchy-looking. He's been doing an excellent job with the poker face—basically not twitching a single muscle throughout the game. His face is so expressionless that I wonder if he might've gotten Botox to help maintain such a stony countenance. His hand is on the table, protectively covering the cards dealt to him.

I move his limp hand away. It feels normal. Well, in a manner of speaking. The hand is sweaty and hairy, so moving it aside is unpleasant and is admittedly an abnormal thing to do. The normal part is that the hand is warm, rather than cold. When I was a kid, I expected people to feel cold in the Quiet, like stone statues.

With the Professional's hand moved away, I pick up his cards. Combined with the king that was hanging in the air, he has a nice high pair. Good to know.

I walk over to Grandma. She's already holding her cards, and she has fanned them nicely for me. I'm able to avoid touching her wrinkled, spotted hands. This is a relief, as I've recently become conflicted about touching people—or, more specifically, women—in the Quiet. If I had to, I would rationalize touching Grandma's hand as harmless, or at least not creepy, but it's better to avoid it if possible.

In any case, she has a low pair. I feel bad for her. She's been losing a lot tonight. Her chips are dwindling. Her losses are due, at least partially, to the fact that she has a terrible poker face. Even before looking at her cards, I knew they wouldn't be good because I could tell she was disappointed as soon as her hand was dealt. I also caught a gleeful gleam in her eyes a few rounds ago when she had a winning three of a kind.

This whole game of poker is, to a large degree, an exercise in reading people—something I really want to get better at. At my job, I've been told I'm great at reading people. I'm not, though; I'm just good at using the Quiet to make it seem like I am. I do want to learn how to read people for real, though. It would be nice to know what everyone is thinking.

What I don't care that much about in this poker game is money. I do well enough financially to not have to depend on hitting it big gambling. I don't care if I win or lose, though quintupling my money back at the blackjack table was fun. This whole trip has been more about going gambling because I finally *can*, being twenty-one and all. I was never into fake IDs, so this is an actual milestone for me.

Leaving Grandma alone, I move on to the next player—the Cowboy. I can't resist taking off his straw hat and trying it on. I wonder if it's possible for me to get lice this way. Since I've never been able to bring back any inanimate objects from the Quiet, nor otherwise affect the real world in any lasting way, I figure I won't be able to get any living critters to come back with me either.

Dropping the hat, I look at his cards. He has a pair of aces—a better hand than the Professional. Maybe the Cowboy is a professional, too. He has a good poker face, as far as I can tell. It'll be interesting to watch those two in this round.

Next, I walk up to the deck and look at the top cards, memorizing them. I'm not leaving anything to chance.

When my task in the Quiet is complete, I walk back to myself. Oh, yes, did I mention that I see myself sitting there, frozen like the rest of them? That's the weirdest part. It's like having an out-of-body experience.

Approaching my frozen self, I look at him. I usually avoid doing this, as it's too unsettling. No amount of looking in the mirror—or seeing videos of yourself on YouTube—can prepare you for viewing your own three-dimensional body up close. It's not something anyone is meant to experience. Well, aside from identical twins, I guess.

It's hard to believe that this person is me. He looks more like some random guy. Well, maybe a bit better than that. I do find this guy interesting. He looks cool. He looks smart. I think women would probably consider him good-looking, though I know that's not a modest thing to think.

It's not like I'm an expert at gauging how attractive a guy is, but some things are common sense. I can tell when a dude is ugly, and this frozen me is not. I also know that generally, being good-looking requires a symmetrical face, and the statue of me has that. A strong jaw doesn't hurt either. Check. Having broad shoulders is a positive, and being tall really helps. All covered. I have blue eyes—that seems to be a plus. Girls have told me they like my eyes, though right now, on the frozen me, the eyes look creepy. Glassy. They look like the eyes of a lifeless wax figure.

Realizing that I'm dwelling on this subject way too long, I shake my head. I can just picture my shrink analyzing this moment. Who would imagine admiring themselves like this as part of their mental illness? I can just picture her scribbling down *Narcissist* and underlining it for emphasis.

Enough. I need to leave the Quiet. Raising my hand, I touch my frozen self on the forehead, and I hear noise again as I phase out.

Everything is back to normal.

The card that I looked at a moment ago—the king that I left on the table—is in the air again, and from there it follows the trajectory it was always meant to, landing near the Professional's hands. Grandma is still eyeing her fanned cards in disappointment, and the Cowboy has his hat on again, though I took it off him in the Quiet. Everything is exactly as it was.

On some level, my brain never ceases to be surprised at the discontinuity of the experience in the Quiet and outside it. As humans, we're hardwired to question reality when such things happen. When I was trying to outwit my shrink early on in my therapy, I once read an entire psychology textbook during our session. She, of course, didn't notice it, as I did it in the Quiet. The book talked about how babies as young as two months old are surprised if they see something out of the ordinary, like gravity appearing to work backwards. It's no wonder my brain has trouble adapting. Until I was ten, the world behaved normally, but everything has been weird since then, to put it mildly.

Glancing down, I realize I'm holding three of a kind. Next time, I'll look at my cards before phasing. If I have something this strong, I might take my chances and play fair.

The game unfolds predictably because I know everybody's cards. At the end, Grandma gets up. She's clearly lost enough money.

And that's when I see the girl for the first time.

She's hot. My friend Bert at work claims that I have a 'type,' but I reject that idea. I don't like to think of myself as shallow or predictable. But I might actually be a bit of both, because this girl fits Bert's description of my type to a T. And my reaction is extreme interest, to say the least.

Large blue eyes. Well-defined cheekbones on a slender face, with a hint of something exotic. Long, shapely legs, like those of a dancer. Dark wavy hair in a ponytail—a hairstyle that I like. And without bangs—even better. I hate bangs—not sure why girls do that to themselves. Though lack of bangs is not, strictly speaking, in Bert's description of my type, it probably should be.

I continue staring at her as she joins my table. With her high heels and tight skirt, she's overdressed for this place. Or maybe I'm underdressed in my jeans and t-shirt. Either way, I don't care. I have to try to talk to her.

I debate phasing into the Quiet and approaching her, so I can do something creepy like stare at her up close, or maybe even snoop in her pockets. Anything to help me when I talk to her.

I decide against it, which is probably the first time that's ever happened.

I know that my reasoning for breaking my usual habit is strange. If you can even call it reasoning. I picture the following chain of events: she agrees to date me, we go out for a while, we get serious, and because of the deep connection we have, I come clean about the Quiet. She learns I did something creepy and has a fit, then dumps me. It's ridiculous to think this, of course, considering that we haven't even spoken yet. Talk about jumping the gun. She might have an IQ below seventy, or the personality of a piece of wood. There can be twenty different reasons why I wouldn't want to date her. And besides, it's not all up to me. She might tell me to go fuck myself as soon as I try to talk to her.

Still, working at a hedge fund has taught me to hedge. As crazy as that reasoning is, I stick with my decision not to phase because I know it's the gentlemanly thing to do. In keeping with this unusually chivalrous me, I also decide not to cheat at this round of poker.

As the cards are dealt again, I reflect on how good it feels to have done the honorable thing—even without anyone knowing. Maybe I should try to respect people's privacy more often. *Yeah, right.* I have to be realistic. I wouldn't be where I am today if I'd followed that advice. In fact, if I made a habit of respecting people's privacy, I would lose my job within days—and with it, a lot of the comforts I've become accustomed to.

Copying the Professional's move, I cover my cards with my hand as soon as I receive them. I'm about to sneak a peek at what I was dealt when something unusual happens.

The world goes quiet, just like it does when I phase in . . . but I did nothing this time.

And at that moment, I see *her*—the girl sitting across the table from me, the girl I was just thinking about. She's standing next to me, pulling her hand away from mine. Or, strictly speaking, from my frozen self's hand——as I'm standing a little to the side looking at her.

She's also still sitting in front of me at the table, a frozen statue like all the others.

My mind goes into overdrive as my heartbeat jumps. I don't even consider the possibility of that second girl being a twin sister or something like that. I know it's her. She's doing what I did just a few minutes ago. She's walking in the Quiet. The world around us is frozen, but we are not.

A horrified look crosses her face as she realizes the same thing. Before I can react, she lunges across the table and touches her own forehead.

The world becomes normal again.

She stares at me from across the table, shocked, her eyes huge and her face pale. She rises to her feet. Without so much as a word, she turns and begins walking away, then breaks into a run a couple of seconds later.

Getting over my own shock, I get up and run after her. It's not exactly smooth. If she notices a guy she doesn't know running after her, dating will be the last thing on her mind. But I'm beyond that now. She's the only person I've met who can do what I do. She's proof that I'm not insane. She might have what I want most in the world.

She might have answers.

CHAPTER TWO

Running after someone in a casino is harder than I imagined, making me wish I'd downed fewer drinks. I dodge elbows and try not to trip over people's feet. I even debate phasing into the Quiet to get my bearings, but decide against it because the casino will still be just as crowded when I phase back out.

Just as I begin to close in on the girl, she turns the corner into a hall leading to the main lobby. I have to get there as quickly as I can, or she'll get away. My heart hammers in my chest as I fleetingly wonder what I'll say to her when I catch up. Before I get far with that thought, two guys in suits step directly into my path.

"Sir," one of the guys says, almost giving me a heart attack. Though I'd spotted them in my periphery, I was so focused on the girl that I hadn't truly registered their presence. The guy who just spoke to me is huge, a mountain in a suit. This can't be good.

"Whatever you guys are selling, I'm not interested," I say, hoping to bluff my way out of this. When they don't look convinced, I add pointedly, "I'm in a rush," and try to look beyond them to emphasize my haste. I hope I look confident, even though my palms are sweating like crazy and I'm panting from my run.

"I'm sorry, but I must insist that you come with us," says the second guy, moving in closer. Unlike his rotund monster of a partner, this guy is lean and extremely buff. They both look like bouncers. I guess they get suspicious when some idiot starts running through the casino. They're probably trained to assume theft or something else shady. Which, to be fair, does make sense.

"Gentlemen," I try again, keeping my voice even and polite, "with all due respect, I really am in a rush. Any way you can frisk me quickly or something? I'm trying to catch up with someone." I add that last part both to deflect suspicion of nefarious activity and because it's the truth.

"You really ought to come with us," the fatter one says, his jaw set stubbornly. They each keep one of their hands near their inner jacket pockets. Oh, great. Just my luck, they're armed.

Struggling to find a way to deal with this unexpected event, I channel the natural fear from my situation into phasing. Once I enter the Quiet, I find myself standing to the side of our not-so-friendly duo, with the world mute again. I immediately resume running, no longer caring about bumping into the immobile people blocking my way. It's not rude to shove them aside here, since they won't know any of this, nor feel anything when the world returns to normal.

When I get to the hall, the girl is already gone, so I move on to the lobby and methodically search for her. Seeing a girl with a ponytail near the elevator, I run over and grab her. As I turn her to get a look at her face, I wonder if my touch will also bring her into the Quiet. I'm pretty sure that's what happened before—she touched me and brought me in.

But nothing happens this time, and the face that looks at me is completely unfamiliar.

Damn it. I've got the wrong person.

My frustration turns to anger as I realize that I lost her because those idiots delayed me at the most critical moment. Fuming, I punch a nearby person with all my strength, needing to vent. As is always the case in the Quiet, the object of my aggression doesn't react in any way. Unfortunately, I don't really feel better either.

Before I decide on my next course of action, I think about what happened at the table. The girl somehow got me to phase into the Quiet, and she was already there. When she saw me, she freaked out and ran. Maybe, like me, this was the first time she's seen anyone 'alive' in there. Everyone reacts differently to strange events, and meeting another person after years of being solo in the Quiet definitely qualifies as strange.

Standing here thinking about it isn't going to get me any answers, so I decide to be thorough and take one more look at the lobby again.

No luck. The girl is nowhere to be found.

Next, I go outside and walk around the casino driveway, trying to see if I can spot her there. I even look inside a few idling cabs, but she's not there either.

Looking up at the flashy building towering over me, I consider searching every room in the hotel. There are at least a couple thousand of them. It would take me a long time, but it might be worth it. I have to find her and get some answers.

Although thoroughly searching a building that

huge seems like a daunting task, it wouldn't be impossible—at least not for me. I don't get hungry, thirsty, or even tired in the Quiet. Never need to use the bathroom either. It's very handy for situations like these, when you need to give yourself extra time. I can theoretically search every room—provided I can figure out how to get in. Those electronic doors won't work in the Quiet, not even if I have the original key from the room's occupants. Technology doesn't usually function here; it's frozen along with everything else. Unless it's something mechanical and simple, like my wind-up watch, it won't work— and even my watch I have to wind every time I'm in the Quiet.

Weighing my options, I try to imagine having to use physical force to break into thousands of hotel doors. Since my iPhone is sadly another technology casualty of the Quiet, I wouldn't even be able to listen to some tunes to kill the time. Even for a cause this important, I'm not sure I want to go to those extremes.

Besides, if I do decide to search the building, now probably isn't the best time to do it. Even if I find her, I won't be able to go after her in the real world thanks to those idiot guards in my way. I need to get rid of them before determining what to do next.

Sighing, I slowly walk back to the hotel. When I

enter the lobby, I scan it again, hoping that I somehow missed her the first time. I feel that same compulsion I get when I lose something around the house. When that happens, I always search the place from top to bottom and then start doing it again— looking in the same places I already checked, irrationally hoping that the third time will be the charm. Or maybe the fourth. I really need to stop doing that. As Einstein said, insanity is doing the same thing over and over again and expecting different results.

Finally admitting defeat, I approach the bouncers. I can spend forever in the Quiet, but when I get out, they'll still be here. There's no avoiding that.

Moving in close, I look in the pocket of the fatter guy to find out what I'm up against. According to his ID, his name is Nick Shifer, and he's with security. So I was right—he's a bouncer. His driver's license is also there, as well as a small family photo. I study both, in case I need the information later.

Next, I turn my attention to the pocket near which Nick's hand is hovering. Looks like I was right again: he has a gun. If I took this gun and shot Nick at close range, he would get a bloody wound and likely fall from the impact. He wouldn't scream, though, and he wouldn't clutch his chest. And when I phase out, he would be whole again, with no signs of damage. It would be like nothing happened.

Don't ask me how I know what happens when you shoot someone in the Quiet. Or stab him. Or hit him with a baseball bat. Or whack him with a golf club. Or kick him in the balls. Or drop bricks on his head—or a TV. The only thing I can say is that I can unequivocally confirm that in a wide variety of cruel and unusual experiments, the subjects turn out to be unharmed once I phase out of the Quiet.

Okay, that's enough reminiscing. Right now, I have a problem to solve, and I need to be careful, with the guns being involved and all.

I smack my frozen self on the back of the head to phase out of the Quiet.

The world unfreezes, and I'm back with the bouncers in real time. I try to look calm, as though I haven't been running around like a crazy man looking for whoever this girl is—because for them, none of that has happened.

"Okay, Nick, I'll be happy to accompany you and resolve this misunderstanding," I say in my most compliant tone.

Nick's eyes widen at hearing his name. "How do you know me?"

"You read the file, Nick," his lean partner says, obviously unimpressed. "The kid is very clever."

The file? What the hell is he talking about? I've never been to this casino before. Oh, and I would love to know how being clever would help someone know the name of a complete stranger on a moment's notice. People always say stuff like that about me, even though it makes no sense. I debate phasing into the Quiet to learn the second guy's name as well, just to mess with them more, but I decide against it. It would be overkill. Instead I decide to mentally refer to the lean guy as Buff.

"Just come with me quietly, please," Buff says. He stands aside, so that he's able to walk behind me. Nick leads the way, muttering something about the impossibility of my knowing his name, no matter how smart I am. He's clearly brighter than Buff. I wonder what he would say if I told him where he lives and that he has two kids. Would he start a cult, or shoot me?

As we make the trek through the casino, I reflect on how knowing things I shouldn't has served me well over the years. It's kind of my thing, and it's gotten me far in life. Of course, it's possible that knowing things I shouldn't is also the reason they have a file on me. Maybe casinos keep records on people who seem to have a history of beating the odds, so to speak.

When we get to the office—a modest-sized room

filled with cameras overlooking different parts of the casino—Buff's first question confirms that theory. "Do you know how much money you won today?" he asks, glaring at me.

I decide to play dumb. "I'm not sure."

"You're quite the statistical anomaly," Nick says. He's clearly proud of knowing such big words. "I want to show you something." He takes a remote from the desk, which has a bunch of folders scattered on its surface. With Nick's press of a button, one of the monitors begins showing footage of me playing at the blackjack table. Watching it, I realize that I did win too much.

In fact, I won just about every time.

Shit. Could I have been any more obvious? I didn't think I'd be watched this closely, but that was stupid of me. I should've taken a couple of hits even when I knew I would bust, just to hide my tracks.

"You're obviously counting cards," Nick states, giving me a hard stare. "There's no other explanation."

Actually, there is, but I'm not about to give it to him. "With eight decks?" I say instead, making my voice as incredulous as possible.

Nick picks up a file on the desk and leafs through it.

"Darren Wang Goldberg, graduated from Harvard with an MBA and a law degree at eighteen. Near-perfect SAT, LSAT, GMAT, and GRE scores. CFA, CPA, plus a bunch more acronyms." Nick chuckles as if amused at that last tidbit, but then his expression hardens as he continues. "The list goes on and on. If anyone could do it, it would be you."

I take a deep breath, trying to contain my annoyance. "Since you're so impressed with my bona fides, you should trust me when I tell you that no one can count cards with eight decks." I have no clue if that's actually true, but I do know casinos have been trying to stack the odds in the house's favor for ages now, and eight decks is too many cards to count even for a mathematical prodigy.

As if reading my mind, Buff says, "Yeah, well, even if you can't do it by yourself, you might be able to pull it off with partners."

Partners? Where did they get the idea that I have partners?

In response to my blank look, Nick hits the remote again, and I see a new recording. This time it's of the girl—of her winning at the blackjack table, then working a number of poker tables. Winning an impressive amount of cash, I might add.

"Another statistical anomaly," Nick says, looking at me intently. "A friend of yours?" He must've worked as a detective before this gig, seeing as how he's pretty good at this interrogation thing. I guess my chasing her through the casino set off some red flags. My reaction was definitely not for the reasons he thinks, though.

"No," I say truthfully. "I've never seen her before in my life."

Nick's face tightens with anger. "You just played at the same poker table," he says, his voice growing in volume with every word. "Then you both started running away just as we were coming toward you. I suppose that's just a coincidence, huh? Do the two of you have someone on the inside? Who else is in on it?" He's full-on yelling at this point, spittle flying in every direction.

This fierce grilling is too much for me, and I phase into the Quiet to give myself a few moments to think.

Contrary to Nick's belief, the girl and I are definitely not partners. Yet it's obvious she was here doing the same thing I was, as the recordings clearly show her winning over and over. That means I didn't have a hallucination, and she really was in the Quiet somehow. She can do what I can. My heart beats faster with excitement as I realize again that I'm not the only one. This girl is like me—which means I really need to find her.

On a hunch, I approach the table and pick up the thickest folder I see.

And that's when I hit the biggest jackpot of the night.

Staring back at me from the file is her picture. Her real name, according to the file, is Mira Tsiolkovsky. She lives in Brooklyn, New York.

Her age shocks me. She's only eighteen. I thought she'd be in her mid-twenties—which would conveniently fit right within my datable age range. As I further investigate the information they've compiled on her, I find the reason I was fooled by her age: she intentionally tries to make herself look older to get into casinos. The folder lists a bunch of her aliases, all of which are banned from casinos. All are aged between twenty-one and twenty-five.

According to the folder, she does this cheating thing professionally. One section details her involvement in cheating both in casinos and underground gambling joints. Scary places by the sound of it, with links to organized crime.

She sounds reckless. I, on the other hand, am most decidedly not reckless. I use my strange ability to make money in the financial industry, which is much safer than what Mira does. Not to mention, the kind of money I bring in through legitimate channels makes the risks of cheating in casinos far outweigh the benefits—especially given what I'm learning today. Apparently casinos don't sit idly by while you take their money. They start files on you if they think you're likely to cheat them, and they blacklist you if you get too lucky. Seems unfair, but I guess it makes business sense.

Returning my attention to the file, I find little personal information beyond her name and address— just other casinos, games, and the amounts she's won under different aliases, plus pictures. She's good at changing her appearance; all the pictures feature women who look very different from one another. Impressive.

Having memorized as much of Mira's file as I can, I walk over to Nick and take my own file from his hands.

I'm relieved to find that there's not much to this folder. They have my name and address, which they must've gotten from the credit card I used to pay for drinks. They know that I work at a hedge fund and that I've never had problems with the law—all stuff easily found on the web. Same goes for Harvard and my other achievements. They probably just did a Google search on me once they knew my name.

Reading the file makes me feel better. They're not on to me or anything like that. They probably just saw me winning too much and decided to nip the situation in the bud. The best thing to do at this point is to placate them, so I can go home and digest all this. No need to search the hotel anymore. I have more than enough information about Mira now, and my friend Bert can help me fill in the rest of the puzzle.

Thus resolved, I walk back to myself. My frozen self's face looks scared, but I don't feel scared anymore because I now have a plan.

Taking a deep breath, I touch my frozen forehead again and phase out.

Nick is still yelling at me, so I tell him politely, "Sir, I'm sorry, but I don't know what or whom you're talking about. I was lucky, yes, but I didn't cheat." My voice quavers on that last bit. I might be overacting now, but I want to be convincing as a scared young man. "I'll be happy to leave the money and never come back to this casino again."

"You *are* going to leave the money, and you won't ever come back to this *city* again," corrects Buff.

"Fine, I won't. I was just here to have fun," I say in a steadier but still deferential voice, like I'm totally in awe of their authority. "I just turned twenty-one and it's Labor Day weekend, so I went gambling for the first time," I add. This should add an air of sincerity, because it's the truth. "I work at a hedge fund. I don't need to cheat for money."

Nick snorts. "Please. Guys like you cheat because you like the rush of being so much smarter than everyone else."

Despite his obvious contempt for me, I don't reply. Every remark I form in my head sounds snide. Instead I just continue groveling, saying that I know nothing, gradually becoming more and more polite. They keep asking me about Mira and about how I cheat, and I keep denying it. The conversation goes in circles for a while. I can tell they're getting as tired of it as I am – maybe more so.

Seeing an opening, I go in for the kill. "I need to know how much longer I'll be detained, sir," I tell Nick, "so that I can notify my family."

The implication is that people will wonder where I am if I don't show up soon. Also, my subtle use of the word 'detained' reminds them of the legality of their position—or more likely, the lack thereof.

Frowning, but apparently unwilling to give in, Nick says stubbornly, "You can leave as soon as you tell us something useful." There isn't much conviction in his voice, though, and I can tell that my question hit the mark. He's just saving face at this point.

Doggedly continuing the interrogation, he asks me the same questions again, to which I respond with the same answers. After a couple of minutes,

Buff touches his shoulder. They exchange a look.

"Wait here," Buff says. They leave, presumably to have a quick discussion out of my earshot.

I wish I could listen in, but sadly it's not possible with the Quiet. Well, that's not entirely true. If I learned to read lips and phased in and out very quickly, I could probably piece together some of the conversation by looking at their frozen faces, over and over again. But that would be a long, tedious process. Plus, I don't need to do that. I can use logic to figure out the gist of what they're saying. I'm guessing it goes something like this: "The kid's too smart for us; we should let him go, get doughnuts, and swing by a strip club."

They return after a few minutes, and Buff tells me, "We're going to let you go, but we don't want to see you—or your girlfriend—here ever again." I can tell Nick isn't happy about having to abandon his questioning without getting the answers he wanted, but he doesn't voice any objections.

I suppress a relieved sigh. I half-thought they'd rough me up or something. It would've sucked, but it wouldn't have been unexpected—or perhaps even undeserved, given that I did cheat. But then again, they have no proof that I cheated. And they probably think I'm clever enough to cause legal problems— particularly given my law degree.

Of course, it's also possible that they know more about me than what's in the file. Maybe they've come across some info about my moms. Oh yeah, did I mention that I have two moms? Well, I do. Trust me, I know how strange that sounds. And before there's any temptation, I never want to hear another joke on the subject. I got enough of that in school. Even in college, people used to say shit sometimes. I usually made sure they regretted it, of course.

In any case, Lucy, who is my adoptive mom—but is nonetheless the most awesome mom ever—is a tough-as-nails detective. If these bozos laid a finger on me, she'd probably track them down and personally kick their asses with a baseball bat. She also has a team that reports to her, and they would likely chime in, too. And Sara, my biological mom—who is usually quite peace-loving—wouldn't stop her. Not in this case.

Nick and Buff are silent as they lead me out of their office and through the casino to the cab waiting area outside.

"If you come here again," Nick says as I get into an empty cab, "I'll break something of yours. Personally."

I nod and quickly close the door. All he had to do was ask me nicely like that. In retrospect, Atlantic City wasn't even that much fun.

I'm convinced I won't ever want to come back.

CHAPTER THREE

I start my post-Labor Day Tuesday morning feeling like a zombie. I couldn't fall asleep after the events at the casino, but I can't skip work today. I have an appointment with Bill.

Bill is my boss, and no one ever calls him that—except me, in my thoughts. His name is William Pierce. As in Pierce Capital Management. Even his wife calls him William—I've heard her do it. Most people call him Mr. Pierce, because they're uncomfortable calling him by his first name. So, yeah, Bill is among the few people I take seriously. Even if, in this case, I'd rather nap than meet with him.

I wish it were possible to sleep in the Quiet. Then I'd be all set. I'd phase in and snooze right under my desk without anyone noticing.

I achieve some semblance of clear thought after my first cup of coffee. I'm in my cubicle at this point. It's eight a.m. If you think that's early, you're wrong. I was actually the last to get into the office in my part of the floor. I don't care what those early risers think of my lateness, though. I can barely function as is.

Despite my achievements at the fund, I don't have an office. Bill has the only office in the company. It would be nice to have some privacy for slacking off, but otherwise, I'm content with my cube. As long as I can work in the field or from home most of the time—and as long as I get paid on par with people who typically have offices—the lack of my own office doesn't bother me.

My computer is on, and I'm looking at the list of coworkers on the company instant messenger. Aha—I see Bert's name come online. This is really early for him. As our best hacker, he gets to stroll in whenever he wants, and he knows it. Like me, he doesn't care what anyone else thinks about it. In fact, he probably cares even less than I do—and thus comes in even later. I initially thought we would talk after my meeting with Bill, but there's no time like the present, since Bert is in already.

"Stop by," I message him. "Need your unique skills."

"BRT," Bert replies. *Be right there.*

I've known Bert for years. Unlike me, he's a real prodigy. We were the only fourteen-year-olds in a Harvard *Introduction to Computer Science* course that year. He aced the course without having to phase into the Quiet and look up the answers in the textbook, the way I did in the middle of the exams. Nor did he pay a guy from Belarus to write his programing projects for him.

Bert is *the* computer guy at Pierce. He's probably the most capable coder in New York City. He always drops hints that he used to work for some intelligence agency as a contractor before I got him to join me here and make some real money.

"Darren," says Bert's slightly nasal voice, and I swivel my chair in response.

Picturing this guy as part of the CIA or FBI always puts a smile on my face. He's around five-four, and probably weighs less than a hundred pounds. Before we became friends, my nickname for Bert was Mini-Me.

"So, Albert, we should discuss that idea you gave me last week," I begin, jerking my chin toward one of our public meeting rooms.

"Yes, I would love to hear your report," Bert

responds as we close the door. He always overacts this part.

As soon as we're alone, he drops the formal colleague act. "Dude, you fucking did it? You went to Vegas?"

"Well, not quite. I didn't feel like taking a five-hour flight—"

"So you opted for a two-hour cab ride to Atlantic City instead," Bert interrupts, grinning.

"Yes, exactly." I grin back, taking a sip of my coffee.

"Classic Darren. And then?"

"They banned me," I say triumphantly, like it's some huge accomplishment.

"Already?"

"Yeah. But not before I met this chick." I pause for dramatic effect. I know this is the part he's really waiting for. His own experience with girls thus far has been horrendous.

Sure enough, he's hooked. He wants to know every detail. I tell him a variation of what happened. Nothing about the Quiet, of course. I don't share that with anyone, except my shrink. I just tell Bert I won a lot. He loves that part, as he was the one who suggested I try going to a casino. This was after he and a bunch of our coworkers got slaughtered by me at a friendly card game.

He, like most at the fund, knows that I know things I shouldn't. He just doesn't know *how* I know them. He accepts it as a given, though. In a way, Bert is a little bit like me. He knows things he shouldn't, too. Only in his case, everyone knows the 'how.' The method behind Bert's omniscience is his ability to get into any computer system he wants.

That is precisely what I need from him now, so as soon I finish describing the mystery girl, I tell him, "I need your help."

His eyebrows rise, and I explain, "I need to learn more about her. Whatever you can find out would be helpful."

"What?" His excitement noticeably wanes. "No, Darren, I can't."

"You owe me," I remind him.

"Yeah, but this is cyber-crime." He looks stubborn, and I mentally sigh. If I had a dollar for every time Bert used that line . . . We both know he commits cyber-crime on a daily basis.

I decide to offer him a bribe. "I'll watch a card trick," I say, making a Herculean effort to inject some enthusiasm into my voice. Bert's attempts at card tricks are abysmal, but that doesn't deter him one bit.

"Oh," Bert responds casually. His poker face is shit, though. I know he's about to try to get more out of me, but it's not going to happen, and I tell him so.

"Fine, fine, text me those aliases you mentioned, the ones that 'fell into your lap,' and the address you 'got by chance,'" he says, giving in. "I'll see what I can do."

"Great, thanks." I grin at him again. "Now I have to go—I've got a meeting with Bill."

I can see him cringing when I call William that. I guess that's why I do it—to get a rise out of Bert.

"Hold on," he says, frowning.

I know what's coming, and I try not to look too impatient.

Bert is into magic. Only he isn't very good. He carries a deck of cards with him wherever he goes, and at any opportunity—real or imaginary—he whips the cards out and tries to do a card trick.

In my case, it's even worse. Because I showed off to him once, he thinks I'm into magic too, and that I only pretend I'm not. My tendency to win when playing cards only solidifies his conviction that I'm a closet magician.

As I promised him, I watch as he does his trick. I won't describe it. Suffice it to say, there are piles of cards on the conference room table, and I have to make choices and count and spell something while turning cards over.

"Great, good one, Bert," I lie as soon as my card is found. "Now I really have to go."

"Oh, come on," he cajoles. "Let me see your trick one more time."

I know it'll be faster for me to go along with him than to argue my way out of it. "Okay," I say, "you know the drill."

As Bert cuts the deck, I look away and phase into the Quiet.

As soon as the world freezes, I realize how much ambient noise the meeting room actually has. The lack of sound is refreshing. I feel it more keenly after being sleep-deprived. Partly because most of the 'feeling like crap' sensation dissipates when I'm in the Quiet, and partly because outside the Quiet, the sounds must've been exacerbating a minor headache that I only now realize is there.

Walking over to motionless Bert, I take the pile of cards in his hand and look at the card he cut to. Then I phase back out of the Quiet.

"Seven of hearts," I say without turning around. The sounds are back, and with them, the headache.

"Fuck," Bert says predictably. "We should go together. Get ourselves banned from Vegas next time."

"For that, I'll need a bigger favor." I wink at him and go back to my cubicle.

When I get to my desk, I see that it's time for my meeting. I quickly text Bert the information he needs to search for Mira and then head off to see Bill.

* * *

Bill's office looks as awesome as usual. It's the size of my Tribeca apartment. I've heard it said that he only has this huge office because that's what our clients expect to see when they visit. That he allegedly is egalitarian and would gladly sit in a cube with low walls, like the rest of us.

I'm not sure I buy that. The decorations are a little too meticulous to support that theory. Plus, he strikes me as a guy who likes his privacy.

One day I'll have an office too, unless I decide to retire first.

Bill looks like a natural-born leader. I can't put my finger on what attributes give this impression. Maybe it's his strong jaw, the wise warmth in his gaze, or the way he carries himself. Or maybe it's something else entirely. All I know is he looks like someone people would follow—and they do.

Bill earned major respect from me when he

played a part in legalizing gay marriage in New York. My moms have dreamed of getting married for as long as I can remember, and anyone who helps make my moms happier is a good person in my book.

"Darren, please sit," he says, pulling his gaze from his monitor as I walk in.

"Hi William, how was your weekend?" I say. He's probably the only person in the office I bother doing the small-talk thing with. Even here, I ask mainly because I know Bill's answer will be blissfully brief. I don't care what my coworkers do in general, let alone on their weekends.

"Eventful," he says. "How about you?"

I try to beat his laconic response. "Interesting."

"Great." Like me, Bill doesn't seem interested in probing beyond that. "I have something for you. We're thinking about building a position in FBTI."

That's the ticker for Future Biotechnology and Innovation Corp; I've heard of them before. "Sure. We need a position in biotech," I say without blinking. In truth, I haven't bothered to look at our portfolio in a while. I just can't recall having biotech-related assignments recently—so I figure there can't be that many biotech stocks in there.

"Right," he says. "But this isn't just to diversify."

I nod, while trying to look my most serious and

thoughtful. That's easier to do with Bill than with most other people. Sometimes I genuinely find what he says interesting.

"FBTI is going to unveil something three weeks from now," he explains. "The stock is up just based on speculation on the Street. It could be a nice short if FBTI disappoints—" he pauses for emphasis, "—but I personally have a hunch that things will go in the other direction."

"Well, to my knowledge, your hunches have never been wrong," I say. I know it sounds like I'm ass-kissing, but it's the truth.

"You know I never act on hunch alone," he says, doing this weird quirking thing he often does with his eyebrow. "In this case, maybe a hunch is understating things. I had some of FBTI's patents analyzed. Plenty of them are for very promising developments."

I'm convinced that I know where this is leading.

"Why don't you poke around?" he suggests, proving my conviction right. "Speak with them and see if the news is indeed bigger than what people are expecting. If that's the case, we need to start building the position."

"I'll do what I can," I say.

This generates a smile from Bill. "Was that humility? That would be a first," he says, seemingly amused. "I need you to do your usual magic. You're up for the challenge, right?"

"Of course. Whatever the news is, you'll know by the end of the week. I guarantee it." I don't add 'or your money back.' That would be too much. What if I get nothing? Bill is the type of person who would hold me to the claim.

"The sooner the better, but we definitely need it before the official news in three weeks," Bill says. "Now, if you'll excuse me."

Knowing that I'm dismissed, I leave him with his computer and go to my cube to make a few phone calls.

As soon as they hear the name Pierce, FBTI is happy to talk to me. I make an appointment with their CTO and am mentally planning the subway trip to their Manhattan office in SoHo when Bert pings me on Instant Messenger.

"Got it," the message says.

"Walk out with me?" I IM back.

He agrees, and we meet by the elevator.

"This chick is crazy," Bert says as I press the button for the lobby. "She leads a very strange life."

Outside his card tricks, Bert knows how to build suspense. I have to give him that. I don't rush him, or else this will take longer. So I just say, "Oh?"

"For starters, you're lucky you have me," he says, his voice brimming with excitement. "She's long gone from that address you found 'by chance.' From what I can puzzle out, that name—Mira—is her real one. Only that name disappeared from the face of the planet a little over a year ago. No electronic trail at all. Same thing with some of those aliases."

"Hmm," I say, giving him the encouragement I know he needs to keep going.

"Well, to get around that, I hacked into some Vegas casino databases, going on the assumption that she would play there as well as in Atlantic City, and sure enough, they had files on some of the other aliases that you mentioned. They also had additional names for her."

"Wow," is all I can say.

"Yeah," Bert agrees. "At first, only one led to any recently occupied address. She's clearly hiding. Anyway, that one alias, Alina something, had a membership at a gym on Kings Highway and Nostrand Avenue, in Brooklyn. Hacking into their system, I found out that the membership is still used sometimes. Once I had that, I set a radius around that gym. People don't usually go far to get workouts."

"Impressive," I say, and mean it. At times like this, I wonder if the business about him being a contractor for some intelligence agency is true after all.

"Anyway, at first there was nothing," he continues. "None of the aliases rent or own any apartments or condos nearby. But then I tried combining first names of some of these aliases with the last names of others." He pauses and looks at me —to get a pat on the back, I think.

"That's diabolical," I say, wishing he would get to the point already.

"Yes," he says, looking pleased. "I am, indeed . . . She, on the other hand, isn't very imaginative. One of the combinations worked. She's partial to the first name of Ilona. Combining Ilona with a last name of Derkovitch, from the Yulia Derkovitch alias, yielded the result I was looking for."

I nod, urging him on.

"Here's that address," he says, grinning as he hands me a piece of paper. Then he asks more seriously, "Are you really going there?"

That's an excellent question. If I do, she'll think I'm a crazy stalker. Well, I guess if you think about it, I am kind of stalking her, but my motives are noble. Sort of.

"I don't know," I tell Bert. "I might swing by that gym and see if I can 'bump into her.'"

"I don't think that will work," he says. "According to their database, her visits are pretty sporadic."

"Great." I sigh. "In that case, yes, I guess I'll show up at her door."

"Okay. Now the usual fine print," Bert says, giving me an intense stare. "You didn't get this from me. Also, the name I found could be a complete coincidence, so it's within the realm of possibility that you might find someone else there."

"I take full responsibility for whatever may occur," I tell Bert solemnly. "We're even now."

"Okay. Good. There's just one other thing . . ."

"What?"

"Well, you might think this is crazy or paranoid, but—" he looks embarrassed, "—I think she might be a spy."

"What?" This catches me completely off-guard.

"Well, something else I should've said is that she's an immigrant. A Russian immigrant, in case you didn't get it from the unusual-sounding names. Came here with her family about a decade ago. When combined with these aliases . . . You see how I would think along these lines, don't you?"

"Right, of course," I say, trying to keep a straight face. A spy? Bert sure loves his conspiracy theories.

"Leave it with me," I say reassuringly. "If she's a spy, I'll deal with it. Now let me buy you a second breakfast and a cup of tea. After that, I'm off to SoHo to meet with FBTI."

CHAPTER FOUR

I make the trip to SoHo. The security guard at the FBTI building lets me in once he knows I have an appointment with Richard Stone, the CTO.

"Hi Richard, I'm Darren. We spoke on the phone." I introduce myself to a tall bald man when I'm seated comfortably in a guest chair in his office. The office is big, with a massive desk with lots of drawers, and a small bookshelf. There's even a plasma TV mounted on the wall. I take it all in, feeling a hint of office envy again.

"Please call me Dick," he says. I have to use every ounce of my willpower not to laugh. If I had a bald head, I'd definitely prefer Richard. In fact, I think I'd prefer to be called Richard over Dick regardless of how I looked.

"Okay, Dick. I'm interested in learning about what you guys are working on these days," I say, hoping I don't sound like I relish saying his nickname too much.

"I'm happy to discuss anything outside of our upcoming announcement," he says, his tone dickish enough to earn that moniker.

I show interest in the standard stuff he's prepared to say, and he goes on, telling me all the boring details he's allowed to share. He continues to talk, but I don't listen. Tuning people out was one of the first things I mastered in the corporate world. Without that, I wouldn't have survived a single meeting. Even now, I have to go into the Quiet from time to time to take a break, or I'd die from boredom. I'm not a patient guy.

Anyway, as Dick goes on, I surreptitiously look around. It's ironic that I'm doing exactly the opposite of what everyone thinks I do. People assume I ask pointed questions of these executives, and figure things out based on their reactions, body language, and who knows what else.

Being able to pick up on body cues and other nonverbal signals is something I want to learn at some point. I even gave it a try in Atlantic City. But in this case, as usual, I rely on something that depends far less on interpretive skills.

When I've endured enough bullshit from Dick, I try to invoke a frightened state of being so I can phase into the Quiet.

Simply thinking myself crazy is not that effective anymore. Picturing myself showing up like a dumbass at that Brooklyn address Bert gave me for Mira, on the other hand—that works like a charm.

I phase in, and Dick is finally, blissfully, quiet. He's frozen mid-sentence, and I realize, not for the first time, that I would have a huge edge if I were indeed able to read body cues. I recognize now that he's looking down, which I believe is a sign that someone's lying.

But no, instead of body language, I read literal language.

I begin with the papers on his desk. There's nothing special there.

Next, I roll his chair, with his frozen body in it, away from the desk. I love it when people in the Quiet are sitting in chairs with wheels. Makes this part of my job easier. In college, I realized I could get the contents of the final exams early by reaching into the professor's desk or bag in the Quiet. Moving the professors aside, though, had been a pain. Their chairs didn't have wheels like corporate office chairs do.

Thinking of those days in school makes me smile, because the things I learned in college are genuinely helpful to me now. This snooping in the Quiet—which is how I finished school so fast and with such good grades—is how I make a living now, and quite a good living at that. So, in some ways, my education really did prepare me for the workforce. Few people can say that.

With Dick and his chair out of the way, I turn my attention to his desk. In the bottom drawer, I hit the mother lode.

FBTI's big announcement will be about a device that will do something called 'transcranial magnetic stimulation.' I vaguely remember hearing about it. Before I delve deeper into the folder I found, I look at the bookshelf. Sure enough, on the shelf is something called *The Handbook of Transcranial Magnetic Stimulation*. It's funny. Now that I know what I'm looking for, I realize that aside from reading body language and cues like that, someone doing this 'for real' likely would've noticed this book on the shelf as a clue to what the announcement would be. In fact, the shelf contains a couple more books on this subject. Now that I think about it, I notice they have less dust on them than the other books on the shelf. Sherlock Holmes would've been proud of my investigative method—only my method works backwards. He used the skill of deductive reasoning, putting the clues he observed together to develop a conclusion. I, however, find evidence to support my conclusion once I know what the answer is.

Returning to my quest for information about the upcoming announcement, I read the first textbook I noticed on the subject. Yes, when I have to—or want to—I can learn the more traditional way. Just because I cheated when it came to tests doesn't mean I didn't legitimately educate myself from time to time. In fact, I did so quite often. However, my education was about whatever I was interested in at the moment, not some cookie-cutter program. I cheated simply because I was being pragmatic. The main reason I was at Harvard was to get a piece of paper that would impress my would-be employers. I used the Quiet to attain the mundane requirements of my degree while genuinely learning about things important to me.

When I do decide to read, the Quiet gives me a huge edge. I never get drowsy, even if the material is a little dry. I don't need sleep in the Quiet, just like I'm not a slave to other bodily functions in there. To me, it feels like it took maybe an hour to finish the part of the book about the magnetic version of stimulation—and it was actually interesting in certain parts. I even skimmed a few other stimulation types, which seem invasive compared to TMS, as the book calls it. I didn't absorb it all, of course—that would require re-reading—but I feel sufficiently ready to tackle the rest of the folder I found in Dick's desk.

I catch myself writing the report to Bill in my head. In layman's terms, TMS is a way to directly stimulate the brain without drilling into the skull—which the other methods require. It uses a powerful magnetic field to do so—hence the 'Magnetic' in the name. It's been around for a while, but was only recently approved by the FDA for treating depression. In terms of harm—and this is not from the book but my own conjecture— it doesn't seem worse than getting an MRI.

It takes me only a brief run through the papers in the folder to realize that the FBTI announcement will exceed everyone's expectations. They have a way of constructing a TMS machine that is more precise than any before, while being affordable and easily customizable. Just for the treatment of depression alone, this device will make a significant impact. To top it off, the work can also lead to better MRI machines, which may open up a new market for FBTI.

Realizing I have enough information, I phase out.

Dick's voice is back. I listen to his closing spiel; then I thank him and go home.

I log in to work remotely, and write up my report in an email. I list all the reasons I think we should go long FBTI and my miscellaneous thoughts on why it would be a good investment.

I set the delivery of my email for late Friday evening. It's a trick I use sometimes to make it appear to my boss and coworkers that I work tirelessly, even on a Friday night, when most people go out or spend time with their families. I copy as many people as is reasonable and address it to Bill. Then I click send and verify that the email is waiting in my outbox. It'll sit there ready and waiting until it goes out Friday night.

Given how much money I'm about to make for Pierce Capital Management, I decide to take the rest of this week off.

CHAPTER FIVE

Showing up uninvited is not the only thing that makes me nervous about my plan to visit Mira. Another thing that worries me is the fact that the address in question happens to be in Brooklyn.

Why do people do that? Why live in the NYC boroughs? My moms are guilty of this as well—their choice, Staten Island, is even crazier. At least the subway goes to Brooklyn. Nothing goes to Staten Island, except the ferry and some express buses. It's even worse than New Jersey.

Still, I don't have a choice. Brooklyn is the location of the address, so off to Brooklyn I go. With deep reservations, I catch the Q train at City Hall and prepare for the epic journey.

As I sit on the subway, I read a book on my phone and occasionally look out the window. Whenever I do, I see graffiti on the walls of buildings facing the tracks. Why couldn't this girl live someplace more civilized, like the Upper East Side?

To my surprise, I get to my stop, Kings Highway, in less than an hour. From here, it's a short walk to my destination, according to my phone's GPS.

The neighborhood is . . . well, unlike the city. No tall buildings, and the signs on businesses are worn and tacky. Streets are a little dirtier than Manhattan, too.

The building is on East 14th Street, between Avenues R and S. This is the only aspect of Brooklyn I appreciate. Navigating streets named using sequential numbers and letters in alphabetical order is easy.

It's late in the afternoon, so the sun is out, but I still feel unsafe—as though I'm walking at night under an ominous-looking, ill-lit bridge in Central Park. My destination is across a narrow street from a park. I try to convince myself that if people let their children play in that park, it can't be *that* dangerous.

The building is old and gloomy, but at least it's not covered in graffiti. In fact, I realize I haven't seen any since I got off the train. Maybe my judgment of the neighborhood was too hasty.

Nah, probably not. It *is* Brooklyn.

The building has an intercom system. I gather my courage and ring the apartment door from downstairs.

Nothing.

I start pressing buttons randomly, trying to find someone who might let me in. After a minute, the intercom comes alive with a loud hiss and a barely recognizable, "Who's there?"

"UPS," I mumble. I'm not sure if it's the plausibility of my lie or someone just working on autopilot, but I get buzzed in.

Spotting an elevator, I press the up arrow, but nothing happens. No light comes on. No hint that anything is working.

I wait for a couple of minutes.

No luck.

I grudgingly decide to schlep to the fifth floor on foot. Looks like my assessment of the neighborhood was spot on after all.

The staircase has an unpleasant odor to it. I hope it's not urine, but my nose suggests it is. The noxious aroma on the second floor is diluted by the smells of boiled cabbage and fried garlic. There isn't a lot of light, and the marble steps seem slippery. Watching my step, I eventually make it to the fifth floor.

It's not until I'm actually staring at the door of 5E that I realize I don't have a good plan. Or any plan at all, really. I came this far, though, so I'm not about to turn around and go home now. I go ahead and ring the doorbell. Then I wait. And wait. And wait.

After a while, I hear some movement inside the apartment. Focusing, I watch the eyehole, the way I've seen people do in the movies.

Maybe it's my imagination, but I think a shadow comes across it. Someone might be looking at me.

Still no response.

I try knocking.

"Who is this?" says a male voice.

Shit. Who the hell is that? A husband? A boyfriend? Her father? Her pimp? Every scenario carries its own implications, and few promise anything good. None I can think of, actually.

"My name is Darren," I say, figuring that honesty is the best policy.

No answer.

"I'm a friend of Mira's," I add. And it's only when the words leave my mouth that I recall that she lives here under a different name. Ilona or something.

Before I can kick myself for the slip, the door swings open. A guy who appears to be a few years older than me stands there looking at me with tired, glassy eyes.

It takes a moment for me to notice one problem. No, make that one huge problem.

The guy is holding a gun.

A gun that looks bigger than his head.

The fear that slams my system is debilitating. I've never been threatened with a gun before. At least, not directly like this. Sure, the bouncers in Atlantic City had guns, but they weren't aiming them in my direction at point-blank range. I never imagined it would be this frightening.

I phase into the Quiet, almost involuntarily.

Now that I'm looking at my frozen self with a gun to his/my face, the panic is diluted. I'm still worried, though, since I am facing the gun in the real world.

I take a deep breath. I need to figure out my plan of action.

I look at the shooter.

He's tall, skinny. He's wearing glasses and a white coat with a red stain on it.

The white coat looks odd—and is that red spot blood, or something else? Questions race through my mind. Who is he? What is he doing in there that requires a gun? Is he cooking meth? It *is* Brooklyn after all.

At the same time, I can't shake the feeling that the guy does not look like an average street criminal. There is keen intelligence in his eyes. His uncombed hair and the pens and ruler in the pocket of his white coat paint a strange picture. He almost looks like a scientist—albeit on the mad side.

Of course, that does not rule out the drug angle. He could be like the character on that show about a teacher who cooks meth. Although, come to think of it, that same show made it clear that you don't do that in an apartment building. The smell is too strong to keep the operation hidden, or something like that.

Now that I've had some time to calm down in the Quiet, I get bolder. I begin to wonder if the gun is real. Or maybe I'm just hoping it's fake. Gathering my courage, I reach out to take it from the guy's hand.

When my fingers touch his, something strange happens. Or stranger, rather.

There are now two of him.

I look at the picture, and my jaw proverbially drops.

There is a second guy in the white coat, right there, and this one is moving. I'm so unaccustomed to the idea of people moving while I'm in the Quiet that I lose my ability to think, so I just stand there and gape at him.

The guy looks at me with an expression that's hard to read, a mixture of excitement and fear. As if I were a bear standing in the middle of a Brooklyn apartment building hall.

"Who are you?" he breathes, staring at me.

"I'm Darren," I repeat my earlier introduction, trying to conceal my shock.

"Are you a Reader, Darren?" the guy asks, recovering some of his composure. "Because if you're a Pusher, I will unload that gun in your face as soon as we Universe Split, or Astral Project, or Dimension Shift, or whatever it is you people call it. As soon as we're back to our bodies, you're dead, Pusher."

He has an unusual accent—Russian, I think. That reminds me of Bert's theory that Mira is a spy. Maybe he was right. Maybe she travels with a whole gang of Russian spies.

I only understand one thing about what the Russian guy is saying: he knows that I'm at his mercy when we get back. That means that he, like me, understands how the Quiet works.

The terms he's using sort of make sense to me. All except 'Reader' and 'Pusher.' I know that even if I were this 'Pusher,' I wouldn't want to admit it and get shot. He probably realizes that as well.

"I am sorry, I don't know what you're talking about," I admit. "I don't know what a Reader or a Pusher is."

"Right," the guy sneers. "And you're not aware of our bodies standing over there?"

"Well, yeah, of that I'm painfully aware—"

"Then you can't expect me to believe that you can Split, but not be one of us—or one of them." He says that last word with disgust.

Okay, so one thing is crystal clear: Reader is good, Pusher is bad. Now if only I could find out why.

"If I were a Pusher, would I just show up here like this?" I ask, hoping I can reason with him.

"You fuckers are clever and extremely manipulative," he says, looking me up and down. "You might be trying to use some kind of reverse psychology on me."

"To what end?"

"You want me dead, that's why, and you want my sister dead too," he says, his agitation growing with every word.

I make a mental note at the mention of 'sister,' but I don't have time to dwell on it. "Would showing up like this be the best way to kill you?" I try to reason again.

"Well, no. In fact, I've never heard of Pushers

doing their dirty work themselves," he says, beginning to look uncertain. "They like to use regular people for that, like puppets."

I have no idea what he's referring to, so I continue my attempts at rational discourse. "So isn't it possible that I'm simply a guy searching for answers?" I suggest. "Someone who doesn't know what you're talking about?"

"No," he says after considering it for a moment. "I've never heard of untrained, unaffiliated people with the ability to Split. So why don't you tell me what you're doing here, outside my door."

"I can explain that part," I say hurriedly. "You see, I met a girl in Atlantic City. A girl who made me realize that I'm not crazy."

At the mention of Atlantic City, I have his full attention. "Describe her," he says, frowning.

I describe Mira, toning down her sex appeal.

"And she told you her name and where she lives?" he asks, clearly suspicious.

"Well, no," I admit. "I was detained by the casino when they thought we were working together to cheat the house. I learned a few of her aliases from them. After that, I got help from a friend who's a very good hacker."

There I go again, using honesty. I'm on a roll. I

don't think I've ever said this many truthful statements in such a short time.

"A good hacker?" he asks, looking unexpectedly interested.

"Yes, the best," I reply, surprised. That's the completely wrong thing to focus on in this story, but as long as he's not angry and trigger-happy, I'll stick with the subject.

He looks me straight in the eyes for the first time. He seems uncomfortable with this. I can tell he doesn't do it often.

I hold his gaze.

"Here's the deal, Darren," he says, his eyes shifting away again after a second. "We're going to get back. I won't shoot you. Instead I will snap your picture. Then I'll text it to my sister."

"Okay," I say. I'll take a picture over a bullet any day.

"If you do anything to me before she gets here, she'll have proof that you were here," he elaborates.

"That makes sense," I lie. So far, there's very little of this that makes any sense at all. "Do whatever you think will help us resolve this misunderstanding."

"The only way to resolve it is to get proof that you're not a Pusher."

"Then let's get that proof," I say, hoping I'll get

bonus points for my willingness to cooperate.

"Okay," he says, and I can tell that his mood is improving. "You must agree to submit to a test, then. Or a couple of tests, actually."

"Of course," I agree readily. Then, remembering the red stain on his coat, I ask warily, "Are they painful, these tests?"

"The tests are harmless. However, if it turns out that you're a Pusher, you better pray my sister isn't here at that point."

I swallow nervously as he continues, "I would just shoot you, you see. But Mira, she might make your death slow and very painful."

I rethink some of my fantasies about Mira. She's sounding less and less appealing. "Let's just do this," I say with resignation.

"Okay. Walk slowly to your body and touch it in such a way that I can clearly see it. Don't Split, or I will shoot you."

If 'Split' is what I think it is—as in phasing into the Quiet—then how would he be able to tell if I did do it? Though it seems unlikely, I decide not to push my luck. Not until I know the results of his tests.

"I'm ready," I say, and demonstratively touch my frozen self on the forehead.

CHAPTER SIX

The sounds are back. There are now only two of us.

He's less intent on shooting me—so I know I didn't just hallucinate our conversation.

As I watch, he reaches into a pocket under his white coat and takes out a phone. Then he snaps a picture of me and writes a text.

"You go first," he says.

I walk into the apartment, the gun pressed to my back, and gape at my surroundings, struck by what I'm seeing.

The place is a mess.

I'm not the kind of guy who thinks it's a girl's job to keep a place neat. But after a certain point, I am the kind of guy who thinks, 'what kind of slob is she?' I'm not sexist, though. I think the guy with the gun to my back is just as responsible for this mess as she is. An episode of that show about hoarders could be filmed here.

Pulling me from my thoughts, the guy makes me go into a room on the left.

It appears to be some kind of makeshift lab—if the lab had a small explosion of wires, empty frozen meal boxes, and scattered papers, that is.

"Sit," he says.

I comply.

He grabs a few cables off the floor, some kind of gizmo, and a laptop, all the while trying to keep the gun pointed at me. Whatever he's setting up is ready in a few minutes.

I realize that the cable things are electrodes. Still holding the gun, he applies them to my temples and a bunch of other places all over my head. I must look like a medusa.

"Okay," he tells me when it's ready. "Split, and then come back."

I'm still so much on edge that phasing into the Quiet is easy. Within an instant, I'm standing next to my frozen body, watching myself. I look ridiculous with all the electrodes.

I momentarily debate snooping through the apartment, but decide against it. Instead I phase back out, anxious to see what's coming next.

The first thing I hear is his laptop beeping.

"Okay," he says after a pause. "Right before you Split, you were at the very least showing an EEG consistent with a Reader."

"I know this is a good thing, but you don't sound too confident," I say. As soon as I say it, I regret it. Reader is good. Why would I say anything that might instill doubt? But I can't help it, because I also want to know more about myself. Getting answers was the whole crazy reason I came here in the first place— well, that, and to confirm I'm not alone.

He looks around the room, then finds a nook to put the gun in. I think this officially means he's warmed up to me.

"I've only tested myself extensively, and have run preliminary tests on my sister," he says, glancing at me again. "I have my father's notes, but I'm not confident this is conclusive. Aside from that, I have no idea if Pushers would have the same EEG results." He furrows his brows. "In fact, it's quite likely they might."

His trust is like a yo-yo. "Isn't there a better test you can do?" I say before he reaches for the gun again.

"There is," he says. "You can actually try to Read."

I keep any witty responses related to reading books to myself. "Will you at least tell me what Readers and Pushers are?" I ask instead.

"I can't believe you don't know." He squints at me suspiciously. "Haven't your parents told you anything?"

"No," I admit, frustrated. "I have no idea what you mean or what parents have to do with anything." I hate not knowing things, did I mention that?

He stares at me for a few moments, then sighs and walks up to me. "My name is Eugene," he says, extending his hand to me.

"Nice to meet you, Eugene." I shake his hand, relieved by this rather-civilized turn of events.

"Listen to me, Darren." His face softens a bit, his expression becoming almost kind. "If what you say is true, then I'll help you." He raises his hand to stop me from thanking him, which I was about to do. "But only if you turn out to be a Reader."

I have never wished to be part of a clique so badly in my life.

"How?" I ask.

"I'll teach you," he says. "But if it fails, if you can't Read, you have to promise to leave and never come back."

Wow, so now the rules have changed in my favor. I won't be killed, even if I'm this Pusher thing. Nice.

"We need to hurry," he adds. "My sister's on the way. If you're a Pusher, she won't care about your situation."

"Why?" I ask. In the list of pros and cons as to whether or not I should date Mira, the cons are definitely in the lead.

"Because Pushers had our parents killed," he says. The kind expression vanishes. "In front of her."

"Oh, I'm so sorry," I say, horrified. I had no idea Mira had gone through something so awful. Whoever these Pushers are, I can't blame her for hating them—not if they killed her family.

Eugene's face tightens at my platitude. "If you're a Pusher and she catches you here, you'll be sorry."

"Right, okay." I get that point now. "Let's find out quickly then."

"Put this on your fingers," Eugene says, and grabs another cable from the shelf.

I put the device on. It reminds me of a heart-rate monitor, the kind a nurse would use on you at a hospital.

Eugene starts something on his laptop and turns the computer toward me.

There's a program on the screen that seems to be tracking my heart rate, so my theory was probably right.

"That's a photoplethysmograph," he says. When he sees my blank stare, he adds, "How much do you know about biofeedback?"

"Not much," I admit. "But I do know it's when scientists use electrodes, similar to the ones you used on me before, to measure your brain patterns." I recall reading about it in the context of a new way to control video games in the future, with your mind—as nature clearly intended. Also to beat lie detectors, but that's a long story.

"Good. That's neurofeedback, which is a type of biofeedback," he explains. His voice takes on a professorial quality as he speaks. I can easily picture him teaching at some community college. Glasses, white coat, and all. "This is a simpler feedback." He points at my fingers. "It measures your heart-rate variability."

Another blank stare from me prompts him to explain further.

"Your heart rate can be a window into your internal emotional state. There is a specific state I need you to master. This device should expedite the training." He looks uncertain when he says 'should'—I'm guessing he hasn't done much of this expedited training before.

I don't care, though. From what I know of biofeedback, it's harmless. If it keeps Mira from shooting me, sign me up.

"Anyway, you can read up on the details later. For now, I need you to learn to keep this program in the green." He points to a part of the screen.

It's like a game, then. There's a big red-alert-looking button activated in the right-hand lower corner of the screen. Next to it are blue and green buttons.

"Sync your breath to this," he says, pointing at a little bar that goes up and down. "This is five-in and five-out breathing."

I breathe in sync to the bar for a few minutes. Whatever leftover fear I had evaporates; the technique is rather soothing.

"That's good," he says, pointing at the important lower corner. The red button is gone, and I'm now in the blue. I keep breathing. The green light eludes me.

I see the graph the software keeps of my heart-rate variability. It begins to look more and more even, almost like sine curves. I find it cool—even if I have no idea what that change means in terms of being able to Read.

The feeling this experience evokes is familiar,

mainly because of the synchronous breathing. Lucy, my mom, taught me to do this as a meditation technique when I was a kid. She said it would help me focus. I think she secretly hoped it would reduce my hyperactivity. I loved the technique and still do it from time to time. It's something she told me she learned from one of her old friends on the force—a friend who passed away. You're supposed to think happy thoughts while doing the breathing, according to her teachings. Since I'm thinking of Lucy already, I remember fondly how she told me that she didn't know how to meditate just because she was Asian, which was what I used to think. It was the first lecture I received on cultural stereotypes, but definitely not the last. It's a pet peeve of both of my moms. They have a lot of pet peeves like that, actually.

Thus thinking happy thoughts, I try to ignore the bar, closing my eyes to do the meditation Lucy taught me. Every few seconds, I peek at the screen to see how I'm doing.

"That's it," Eugene says suddenly, startling me. When I open my eyes this time, I see the curves are even straighter, and the button is green.

"You did that much too easily," he says, giving me a suspicious look. "But no matter. Do it again, without looking at the screen at all."

He takes the laptop away, and I do my 'Lucy meditation.' In less than a minute, he looks at me with a more awed expression.

"That is amazing. I haven't heard of anyone reaching Coherence so quickly before on the first try," he says. "You're ready for the real test."

He gets up, gets the gun, and puts it in his lab coat pocket. Then, much to my surprise, he leads me out of the apartment.

I'm especially puzzled when he walks across the hall and rings the doorbell of the neighboring apartment.

The door opens, and a greasy-haired, redheaded young guy looks us over. His eyes are bloodshot and glassy.

Without warning, everything silences.

Eugene is pulling his hand away from my frozen self. He must've done that trick his sister pulled on me at the casino. He must've phased in and touched me, bringing me into the Quiet. It's creepy to think about—someone touching my frozen self the way I've touched so many others—but I guess I need to get used to the idea, since I'm no longer the only one who can do this.

Eugene approaches the guy and touches him on the forehead. I half-expect the guy to appear in the Quiet, too.

But no. There are only five of us: a frozen Eugene and me, the moving versions of us, and this guy, who's still a motionless statue.

I watch, confused, as Eugene just stands there, holding the guy's forehead. He looks so still that he begins to remind me of his frozen self.

Then he starts moving again. His hand is not on the guy's head anymore.

"Okay," he says, pointing at the guy. "Now you do the same thing. Place your hand on his skin."

I walk up to the guy and comply. His forehead is clammy, which is kind of disgusting.

"Okay, now close your eyes and get into that same Coherence state," Eugene instructs.

I close my eyes and start doing the meditation. And then it happens.

* * *

I'm so fucking stoned. That was some good shit Peter sold me. I've gotta get some more.

I feel great, but at the same time a part of myself wonders—why the hell did I smoke pot? My hedge fund does random urine tests on occasion. What if I get tested?

And then it hits me: *I* am not stoned. *We* are

stoned. I, *Darren*, am not. But I, *Nick*, am.

We are Nick right now.

We are listening to "Comfortably Numb" by Pink Floyd, which is also how we feel.

I, Darren, tried pot before. I didn't like it nearly as much as I, Nick, like it right now.

We get a craving, but we're too lazy to get anything to eat.

The doorbell rings.

Wow.

Can that be a delivery? We don't recall ordering, but ordering something—pizza or Chinese—sounds like a great idea right about now. We reach for the phone when the doorbell rings again.

Oh yeah, the door.

Who's at the door? we wonder again, with a pang of paranoia this time.

I, Darren, finally get it: it's Eugene and me ringing the doorbell.

We get up, walk to the door, and open it after fumbling with the locks.

We're looking at Eugene, Mira's older brother, and some other dude, who I, Darren, recognize as myself. We wonder what the deal is.

* * *

Suddenly, I'm standing in the corridor, my hand no longer on Nick's forehead. I stare at Eugene, my mouth gaping and heart racing at the realization of what I just did.

"Eugene, did you want me to get inside this pothead's mind?" I manage to ask. "Is Reading 'Mind Reading'?"

Eugene smiles at me, then walks to his frozen self and touches his own temple, bringing us out of the Quiet. Then he makes some bullshit excuse to confused Nick for ringing the doorbell, and we walk back to Eugene's apartment.

"Tell me everything you just experienced," he says as soon as the door closes behind us.

I tell him. As I go on, his smile widens. He must've seen the same thing when he touched the guy. From his reaction, I guess this means I can Read, and since this apparently removes any suspicions he had about me, I also assume that Pushers can't Read. I think I'm starting to figure out at least a few pieces of the mystery.

This was the test—and incredibly, I passed.

CHAPTER SEVEN

What I did was not exactly how I imagined mind reading—not that mind reading is something I imagined much. The experience was like some kind of virtual reality, only more intense. It was like I was the pothead guy. I felt what he felt. Saw what he saw. I even had his memories, and they came and went as though they were mine.

But at the same time, I was also myself. An observer of sorts. I experienced two conflicted world views. On the one hand, I was Nick, feeling high, feeling numb, feeling dumb, but at the same time, I was myself, able to not lose my own consciousness. It was a strange merger.

I want to do it again—as soon as possible.

"Do you want tea?" Eugene asks, dragging me out of my thoughts, and I realize we somehow ended up at the kitchen table.

I look around the room. There are a bunch of beakers all over the place. Is he running some kind of chemistry experiment in here? A red stain on the counter, near an ampule with remains of that same red substance, matches the stain on Eugene's white coat. At least it's not blood, as I had originally thought.

"I will take your silence as a yes to tea." Eugene chuckles. "I'm sorry," he adds, joining me after setting the kettle on the stove. "The first time we Read is usually not as confusing as that. Nick's intoxicated state must've been an odd addition to an already strange experience."

"That's an understatement," I say, getting my bearings. "So how does this work?"

"Let's begin at the beginning," Eugene says. "Do you now know what a Reader is?"

"I guess. Someone who can do that?"

"Exactly." Eugene smiles.

"And what is a Pusher?"

His smile vanishes. "What Pushers do is horrible. An abomination. A crime against human nature.

They commit the ultimate rape." His voice deepens, filling with disgust. "They mind-rape. They take away a person's will."

"You mean they can hypnotize someone?" I ask, trying to make sense of it.

"No, Darren." He shakes his head. "Hypnosis is voluntary—if the whole thing exists at all. You can't make people do something they don't want to do under hypnosis." He stops at the sound of the kettle. "Pushers can make a person do anything they want," he clarifies as he gets up.

I don't know how to respond, so I just sit there, watching him pour us tea.

"I know it's a lot to process," Eugene says, placing the cup in front of me.

"You do have a gift for stating the obvious."

"You said you came here to get answers. I promised I would provide them. What do you want to know?" he says, and my heart begins to pound with excitement as I realize I'm about to finally learn more about myself.

"How does it work?" I ask before he changes his mind and decides to test me some more. "Why can we phase into the Quiet?"

"Phase into the Quiet? Is that what you call Splitting?" He chuckles when I nod. "Well, prepare to be disappointed. No one knows for sure why we can do it. I have some theories about it, though. I'll tell you my favorite one. How much do you know about quantum mechanics?"

"I'm no physicist, but I guess I know what a well-read layman should know."

"That might be enough. I'm no physicist myself. Physics was my dad's field, and really this is his theory. Have you ever heard of Hugh Everett III?"

"No." I've never heard of the first two either, but I don't say that to Eugene.

"It's not important, as long as you've heard of the multiple universes interpretation of quantum mechanics." He offers me sugar for my tea.

"I think I've heard of it," I say, shaking my head to decline the sugar. Eugene sits across from me at the table, his gaze intent on mine. "It's the alternative to the famous Copenhagen interpretation of quantum mechanics, right?"

"Yes. We're on the right track. Now, do you actually understand the Copenhagen interpretation?"

"Not really. It deals with particles deciding where to be upon observation with only a probability of being in a specific place—introducing randomness into the whole thing. Or something along those lines. Isn't it famous for no one understanding it?"

"Indeed. I doubt anyone really does. Even my dad didn't, which is why he said it was all BS. He would point out how the whole Schrödinger's cat paradox is the best example of the confusion." As he talks, Eugene gets more and more into the conversation. He doesn't touch his tea, completely immersed in the subject. "Schrödinger meant for the cat theory to illustrate the wrongness, or at least the weirdness of that interpretation, which is funny, given how famous the cat example became. Anyway, what's important is that Everett said there is no randomness. Every place a particle can be, it is, but in different universes. His theory is that there is nothing special about observing particles, or cats—that the reality is Schrödinger's cat is both alive and dead, a live cat in one universe and a dead one in another. No magic observation skills required. Do you follow?"

"Yes, I follow," I say. Amazingly enough, I actually do. "I had to read up on this when we wanted to invest in a firm that was announcing advances in quantum computing."

"Oh, good." Eugene looks relieved. "That might expedite my explanation considerably. I was afraid I would have to explain the double-slit experiment and all that to you. You've also heard of the idea that brains might use quantum computing in some way?"

"I have," I say, "but I've also read that it's unlikely."

"Because the temperatures are too high? And the effects are too short-lived?"

"Yeah. I think it was something along those lines."

"Well, my dad believed in it regardless, and so do I. No one really knows for sure, wouldn't you admit?" Eugene says.

I never really thought about it. It's not something that was ever important to me. "I guess so," I say slowly. "I read that there are definitely *some* quantum effects in the brain."

"Exactly." He takes a quick sip of tea and sets it aside again. I do the same. The tea is bitter and too hot, and I'm dying for Eugene to continue. "The unlikelihood that you mention is about whether consciousness is related to quantum effects. No one doubts that some kinds of quantum processes are going on in the brain. Since everything is made of subatomic particles, quantum effects happen everywhere. This theory just postulates that brains are leveraging these effects to their benefit. Kind of like plants do. Have you heard of that?"

"Yes, I have." He's talking about the quantum effects found in the process of photosynthesis. Mom—Sara—emailed me a bunch of articles about that. She's very helpful that way—sending me articles on anything she thinks I might be interested in. Or anything she's interested in, for that matter.

"Photosynthesis evolved over time because some creature achieved an advantage when using a quantum effect. In an analogous way, wouldn't a creature able to do any kind of cool quantum calculations get a huge survival advantage?" he asks.

"It would," I admit, fascinated.

"Good. So the theory is that what we can do is directly related to all this—that we find ourselves in another universe when we Split, and that a quantum event in our brains somehow makes us Split." He looks more and more like a mad scientist when he's excited, as he clearly is now.

"That's a big leap," I say doubtfully.

"Okay, then, let me go at it from another angle. Could brains have evolved an ability to do quick quantum computations? Say in cases of dire emergencies?"

"Yeah, I think that's possible." Evolution is something I know well, since Sara's PhD thesis dealt with it. I've known how the whole process works since second grade.

"Well, then let's assume, for the sake of this theory, that the brain has learned to leverage quantum effects for some specific purpose. And that as soon as the brain does that anywhere in nature, evolution will favor it. Even if the effect is tiny. As long as there's some advantage, the evolutionary change will spread."

"But that would mean many creatures, and all people, have the same ability we do," I say. I wonder if I have someone else who doesn't understand evolution on my hands.

"Right, exactly. You must've heard that some people in deeply stressful life-or-death situations experience time as though it's slowing down. That some even report leaving their bodies in near-death experiences."

"Yes, of course."

"Well, what if that's what it feels like for regular people to do this quantum computation, which is meant to save their lives or at least give their brains a chance to save them? You see, the theory asserts that this *does* happen and that all people have this 'near-death' quantum computation boost. All the anecdotal reports that mention strange things happening to people in dire circumstances confirm it. So far, the theory can be tied back to natural evolution."

"Okay," I say. "I think I follow thus far."

"Good." Eugene looks even more excited. "Now let's suppose that a long time ago, someone noticed this peculiarity—noticed how soldiers talk about seeing their lives pass before their eyes, or how Valkyries decide on the battlefield who lives and who dies ... That person could've decided to do something really crazy, like start a cult—a cult that led to a strange eugenics program, breeding people who had longer and stronger experiences of a similar nature." He stands, tea forgotten, and begins to pace around the room as he talks. "Maybe they put them under stress to hear their stories. Then they might've had the ones with the most powerful experiences reproduce. Over a number of generations, that selective breeding could've produced people for whom this quantum computing under stress was much more pronounced—people who began to experience new things when that overly stressed state happened. Think about it, Darren." He stops and looks at me. "What if we're simply a branch of that line of humanity?"

This theory is unlike anything I expected to hear. It seems farfetched, but I have to admit it makes a weird sort of sense. There are parts that really fit my own experiences. Things that Eugene doesn't even know—like the fact that the first time I phased into the Quiet was when I fell off my bike while somersaulting in the air. It was exactly like the out-of-body experience he described. An experience I quickly discovered I could repeat whenever I was stressed.

"Does this theory explain Reading?" I ask.

"Sort of," he says. "The theory is that everyone's minds Split into different universes under some conditions. As Readers, we can just stay in those universes for a longer period of time, and we're able to take our whole consciousness with us." He draws in a deep breath. "The next part is somewhat fuzzy, I have to admit. If you touch a normal person who's unable to control the Split like we can, they're unaware of anything happening. However, if you touch a Reader or a Pusher—another person like us—while in that other universe, they get pulled in with you. Their whole being joins you, just like I joined you when you touched my hand earlier today. When you touch someone 'normal,' they just get pulled in a little bit—on more of a subconscious level. Just enough for us to do the Reading. Afterwards, they have no recollection of it other than a vague sense of déjà vu or a feeling that they missed something, but even those cases are extremely rare."

"Okay, now the theory sounds more wishy-washy," I tell him.

"It's the best I've got. My dad tried to study this question scientifically and paid the ultimate price."

I stare at Eugene blankly, and he clarifies,

"Pushers killed him for his research."

"What? He was killed for trying to find these answers?" I can't hide my shock.

"Pushers don't like this process being studied," Eugene says bitterly. "Being the cowards that they are, they're afraid."

"Afraid of what?"

"Of 'normal' people learning to do what we do," Eugene says, and it's clear that he's not scared of that possibility.

CHAPTER EIGHT

I sip my tea quietly for a while. Eugene comes back to the table and sits down again, sipping from his own mug. My brain is on information overload. There are so many directions this conversation could go. I have so many questions. I've never met anyone who even knew the Quiet existed, let alone knew this much about it—other than Mira, of course, but chasing someone through a crowded casino doesn't technically qualify as 'meeting.'

"Are there other theories?" I ask after a few moments.

"Many," he says. "Another one I like is the computer simulation one. If you've seen *The Matrix*, it's relatively easy to explain. Only it doesn't answer as many things as the Quantum Universes explanation does. Like the fact that our abilities are hereditary."

I was initially curious about the computer simulation theory, but the heredity angle stops me dead in my tracks.

"Wait, does every Reader have to have Reader parents?" I ask. In hindsight, it's obvious from what he's said thus far, but I want it spelled out.

"Yes." He puts his now-empty teacup down. "Which reminds me. Who are your parents? How could you not have known that you're a Reader?"

"Hold on." I raise my hand. "Both parents must be Readers?"

"No." He looks upset for some reason. "Not both. Just one." It's obvious that this is a sensitive subject for Eugene.

Before I can question him about that, he continues, "I don't understand why your parents didn't tell you about this. I always thought this was an oral tradition, a story that every family who has the ability passes from generation to generation. Why didn't yours?"

"I'm not sure," I say slowly. Sara never told me anything. In fact, it was just the opposite. When I told my moms about falling off that bike and seeing the world from outside my body, they told me I must've hit my head. When I repeated the feat by jumping off a roof and told them of another out-of-body excursion, they got me my first therapist. That therapist eventually ended up referring me to my current shrink—who's the only person I've spoken to about this since then. Well, until I met Eugene, that is.

Eugene gives me a dubious look in response. "Really? Neither your mother nor your father ever mentioned it?"

"Well, I didn't know my father, so he's the more likely candidate, given that my mom never said anything," I say, thinking out loud. Based on the confusion on his face, Eugene isn't getting it. Why would he, though? My history isn't exactly common for your typical American family. "I was conceived through artificial insemination," I explain to him. "My father was a guy who contributed to a sperm bank in Israel. Could he have been one of us—a Reader?"

My genius father. What a joke. I rarely tell people this story. Having two moms can be awkward enough. The fact that Sara went shopping for good sperm to have a smart kid—that's just icing on the cake. But that's exactly what she did. She and Lucy went to Israel, found a high-IQ donor bank, and got one of them knocked up. I think they went overseas to make sure I would never, ever meet the father. Now you can see why I consider my shrink's job too easy. Whatever happens, blame the mother.

"What? No, that can't be," Eugene says, interrupting my ruminations. "It has to be your mother. Giving sperm like that is not something our people would do. It's forbidden."

"What do you mean?"

"We have rules," he says, and it's clear something about this upsets him again. "In the old days, all Readers were subject to arranged marriages—hence the whole selective breeding theory, you see. Today things are more liberal, but there are still a number of restrictions. For example, a Reader's choice of spouse, regardless of how powerful he or she is, is considered personal business now, but the expectation is that he or she be a Reader."

I file away the mention of 'powerful.' I'm curious how one can be more or less powerful when it comes to Reading, but I have other questions first. "Because of the selective breeding thing?" I ask, and Eugene nods.

"Right. It's about the blood. Having children with non-Readers gets you banned from the Reader community." He pauses before saying quietly, "That's what happened to my father."

Now I understand why this is a sensitive topic. "I see. So your mother wasn't a Reader? And that's forbidden?"

"Well, technically, marrying non-Readers and having children like me and Mira is no longer forbidden. You don't get executed for it, like in the old days. It *is* highly frowned upon, though, and the punishment for it is banishment. But that's not an issue in your case. What you're talking about—a Reader giving sperm—is forbidden to this day, as it can lead to mixing of the blood and is untraceable."

"Mixing? Untraceable?" I'm completely confused now.

"A Pusher mother might somehow get impregnated by Reader sperm," Eugene explains. "Readers consider that an abomination, and, according to what my dad told me, so do Pushers. They wouldn't give sperm either. The risk is admittedly infinitesimally small, since Pushers themselves wouldn't dare risk getting pregnant that way. Also, mixing aside, Readers like to keep tabs on everyone, even half-bloods like me, and sperm bank pregnancy would prevent them from keeping an account of the whole Reader family tree. Or at least it would require oversight of the whole process, which would be complicated."

That makes sense. But this leads to only one

logical conclusion. Sara, my biological mother, must be a Reader. How could she keep this from me—her son? How could she pretend I was crazy?

"I'm sorry, Darren," Eugene says when I remain silent. "You must have even more questions than before."

"Yes. Your gift for understatement doesn't fail you," I tell him. "I have hundreds of questions. But you know what? You know what I really want to do?"

"You want to Read again?" he surmises.

He's spot on. "Can we?"

"Sure." He smiles. "Let's ring some doorbells."

CHAPTER NINE

I have to admit, I like Eugene. I'm glad I met him.
It's refreshing to have another smart person to talk
to, besides Bert.

It takes us a few minutes to choose our next
'volunteer,' a tall guy in his mid-twenties who lives a
few doors down from Eugene and Mira.

"Hi Brad," Eugene says. "I ran out of salt as I was
cooking. Mind if I borrow some?"

The guy looks confused. "Salt? Um, okay, sure.
Let me see if I can get some." As he turns away,
Eugene winks at me. As we agreed, I phase in and
touch Eugene's forehead to bring him into the Quiet.

It works, as expected. We are in the Quiet, which I

guess, given Eugene's favorite theory, might be another universe of some kind. I don't dwell on the many questions about this alternate reality, if that's what it is. I have something much more interesting to do. I walk up to Brad, touch his temple with my index finger, and close my eyes.

Then I do the breathing meditation.

* * *

What the fuck? Who runs out of salt? The thoughts running through our mind are less than flattering toward Eugene. And who's this other guy? His boyfriend? Wouldn't surprise us. We always suspected that Mira's geeky brother was gay.

I, Darren, realize that Brad knows both Eugene and Mira. And I know I only have seconds before I play his memory to the current moment, which Eugene told me would force me out of the guy's head. So I try to do something different. As Eugene instructed me earlier, I try to 'fall' deeper into Brad's mind.

I picture myself lighter than air. I visualize myself as a feather, slowly floating down into a calm lake on a windless day. I become a sense of lightness.

And then it happens.

We are in a movie theater. We are on a date. We look at the girl sitting next to us, and I, Darren, can't believe my eyes. We're sitting next to Mira. When we start making out with her, I, Darren, think that maybe I really have gone crazy. But no, there is a simpler explanation. I get it when I try falling deeper again.

We're standing in front of Mira's apartment door holding flowers. "These are for you," we say when she opens the door.

We feel pretty slick. The flowers are a means to an end. We want to get our hot neighbor into bed.

"Oh, how sweet," she says drily when she sees us. "Am I supposed to swoon now?" She then proceeds to tell us exactly what she thinks we're planning. I, Darren, realize that she must've done what I'm doing. She must've Read Brad's mind—or maybe she just used common sense. Why else does a guy give a girl flowers?

We're surprised at our neighbor's bluntness. Impressed, even. We admit that, yes, we want to sleep with her, but that she should still take the flowers. She does. Then she sets the ground rules. Nothing serious. She has no time for relationships, she says. A movie, dinner, and, if she thinks we're worth it afterwards, maybe she'll go to our place. That's it. Just a one-time thing, unless the whole thing goes exceptionally well. In that unexpected eventuality, she might, maybe, initiate another encounter.

We agree. What sane guy wouldn't?

I, Darren, experience the dinner and the movie. It's awesome. All of it.

We get back to our— Brad's— apartment.

We're in the bedroom. We're kissing Mira. I, Darren, am jealous that an asshole like Brad gets to do this with Mira. That feeling doesn't last, though. We're immersed in the experience. Mira's perfect naked body. Her lips on ours. It's everything we ever hoped it would be.

Unfortunately, it's too much of everything we ever hoped it would be. I, Darren, can feel us— Brad—losing control. No amount of baseball stats will pull this guy back from the edge. Just like that, we have a problem. Apparently Mira is a little too good-looking, because before I, Darren, even realize what's going on, things happen somewhat . . . prematurely.

Mira's reaction to the situation is admirable. She's not mad, she insists. She says not to worry about it. Says she had a good time. She isn't fooling us, though. She leaves quickly and never speaks to us about this night, or anything else for that matter, again.

* * *

I'm back in my body in the Quiet, and the first thing I do is punch Brad in the face.

"What are you doing?" Eugene exclaims, looking at me like I'm crazy.

"Trust me," I say, resisting the urge to also kick the guy. What a loser. Not only did he sleep with Mira, he didn't even have the decency to be good at it. "He doesn't feel it. Right?"

"Well, yeah," Eugene admits. "At least I highly doubt he feels it. But it looks disrespectful."

It's almost too bad that Brad can't feel the punch. I debate punching him once we phase out, but decide against it. I mean, what possessed me? Mira isn't my girlfriend to be overprotective about. She might not even like me when we meet. One thing is clear, though. Without having said a word to her in real life, I like her.

It's shallow, I know. I'd like to say it's based on the fact that I liked talking to her as Brad at that dinner—which I did. But truthfully, I just want to see her body again. I have to kiss her again. It's weird. I wish I had been in someone else's mind for this, my second Reading. I wish it hadn't been Brad. I really need to find a boring person whose mind I can do this Reading thing with.

"Let's phase out," I tell Eugene, and without waiting for his answer, I touch my forehead.

The world comes back to life, and Brad brings us the stupid salt. Eugene thanks him, and we walk back toward Eugene's apartment.

"How was that?" Eugene asks on the way.

He has no idea this thing happened between his sister and his neighbor. I decide to respect whatever shred of privacy these two have, and at least not mention anything to Eugene.

"That was a good start," I say. "I think we should go outside and do some more."

"Eugene," a pleasant female voice says. A voice I just heard in Brad's memory. "Who the fuck is this?"

I look up and find myself staring down the barrel of a gun. Again.

CHAPTER TEN

Okay, I am officially sick of guns being pointed at me. Even guns pointed by a beautiful girl I just saw naked in someone's mind.

"Mira, put the gun down," Eugene says. "This is Darren. I just texted you his picture. You didn't get it?"

She frowns, still holding the gun trained on me. "No, I haven't checked my phone. Does your text explain how this creep stalked me all the way here from Atlantic City?"

"No, not exactly," Eugene admits. "But you have to cut the guy some slack. He tracked you down, but he has a good reason to be persistent. You're the first other Reader he's ever met."

I can tell that this knowledge surprises her. "How can I be the first Reader he's met?" she asks skeptically. "What about his parents? What about the other Readers from wherever his home is?"

"Manhattan," I supply helpfully. "And in regards to parents, I'll be having a very serious conversation with my mom about this very subject. For some reason, she didn't tell me anything about this. And I've never met my father, but Eugene convinced me that he couldn't have been a Reader because my mother got his sperm from a bank."

As I'm talking, Mira looks at me with more and more curiosity. "A sperm bank?" she repeats.

"Yes. My mom, she wanted a child, but couldn't bring herself to be with a guy, I guess." Thinking of my mom in this context is weird, at best.

"Why? Does she hate men?"

Did Mira just say that approvingly?

"She likes women," I say. "I have two mothers." I'm not sure why I added this last part. Usually you have to ask probing questions for a lot longer before I reveal such personal information.

To her credit, Mira hardly blinks at that. Instead she says with a frown, "If she got sperm from a bank, that would mean she voluntarily mated with a non-

Reader. Why would she have done that? Surely she knew she'd get exiled, like our dad."

"That's a good point," Eugene says. "I can't believe I didn't see that when Darren first mentioned it to me."

"You say that like you're surprised I could make a good point," Mira says to her brother, but her tone is more teasing than sharp. "Don't forget, you wouldn't survive a day without me—the dumb, uneducated one."

Eugene ignores her statement. "Can we get out of this hallway?" he says. "I want to get something to eat."

Mira finally lowers the gun and puts it back in her purse. "Fine, I'll be right back." She goes into the apartment. I look at Eugene questioningly, but he just shrugs.

She's back momentarily. She changed from her heels and dress into jeans and sneakers. I wonder where she's been, so dressed up. She looks great in the simpler outfit, though, and I can't help thinking back to my experience in Brad's head.

As I'm sifting through the hot pictures in my mind, she tells Eugene, "Are you seriously going out like that?" She gestures toward his stained lab coat.

He mumbles something and disappears into the apartment as well. When he comes out, the lab coat is gone, and he's wearing a long-sleeved T-shirt that looks two sizes too big. Mira shoots him an exasperated look, but doesn't say anything else. Instead she walks over to the elevator and presses the button.

"I don't think that works," I say, remembering having to go up all those stairs.

"Trust me," she says. "It's just the first floor that doesn't work."

And she's right. The elevator comes, and we're able to exit on the second floor. From there, it's only a single flight of stairs to get out of the building.

"What exactly does it mean to be exiled?" I ask as we walk in the direction of the bigger street, Kings Highway, in search of a place to eat.

"It's complicated," Eugene says, looking at me. "Our dad was exiled from the community of Readers in St. Petersburg, Russia, and that was pretty bad. He couldn't visit his childhood friends and family. Readers in Russia, in general, are much more traditional, but it was especially bad almost thirty years ago, when I was born. It was terrible for him, he told us."

"But he did it for Mom," Mira adds.

"And for us. He left it all so he could have children with her." Eugene sounds proud of his father. "Thankfully, it's different here. In present-day

America, especially the New York City area, the Readers' community is more open-minded. They recognize us as Readers—unofficially, at least."

"Yeah, just so they can make sure we don't openly use our skills," Mira says with a touch of bitterness.

"I think they have other ways to enforce that," Eugene says, glancing at his sister. "Besides, we all know how stupid it would be to reveal our existence to the rest of the world, half-bloods or not. No, they're genuinely less traditional here. At least now they are. But when you were born, Darren, things could've been worse." He gives me a sympathetic look.

"None of this explains why my mom didn't tell me about Readers, though," I say, still bothered by the thought of Sara hiding such important information from me.

"Maybe she was ashamed of being shunned," Mira suggests, shooting me a look that suggests she's not entirely over my stalking her. "Or she didn't want you to learn how to Split and Read. Maybe as you were growing up, she decided you wouldn't be able to keep the Readers' secret. No offense, but you don't look like the kind of guy who can keep your mouth shut."

"But she must've realized I'd discovered it. I as much as told her that as a kid," I say, refusing to rise to the bait. I have more important things to worry about than Mira's sharp tongue. I'm tempted to go to Staten Island right now, but I know it makes more sense to learn more from these two first, so I can ask my mom the right questions. Maybe then I'll be able to get answers and understand what happened.

"I'm sorry," Eugene says with a hint of pity.

"Oh, poor Darren, Mommy didn't tell him," Mira counters, her voice dripping with venom. "At least she's alive. Maybe that's why she is alive—because she knows how to keep a secret. She doesn't run around asking troublesome questions like our idiot father." As she says this, her hands ball into fists, and I see her blinking rapidly, as though to hide tears. She doesn't cry, though. Instead, she glares at her brother and says caustically, "The father whose steps you seem determined to follow, I might add."

"I thought you supported my research," Eugene says, clearly hurt.

She sighs and falls silent as we pass through a small crowd gathered in front of some yogurt place. "I'm sorry," she says in a more conciliatory tone when we're through. "I do support what you're doing. I support it to spite the fuckers who killed Dad—and because it could give us a way to make them pay for what they did. I just can't help thinking that all of this could've been avoided if he'd just researched something else. Alzheimer's, for example."

"I understand," Eugene says.

We walk in an uncomfortable silence for a few minutes. I feel like an intruder.

"No offense, Darren," Mira says as we stop at a traffic light. "It's a difficult subject."

"No problem," I say. "I can't even imagine how you feel."

We walk in a more companionable silence for another block or so.

"Are you leading us to that diner again?" Mira eventually asks, wrinkling her nose.

"Yes," Eugene says, a faint smile appearing on his lips.

Mira rolls her eyes. "That place is a real dump. How many cases of food poisoning does it take for you to realize it? Let's go to the sushi place on Coney Island. It's closer."

"Right, raw fish is the solution to health concerns," Eugene says, unsuccessfully trying to mimic Mira's very distinctive brand of sarcasm.

They fight about the place for the rest of the way. I'm not surprised at all when Mira gets her way. She seems like the kind of person who always does. I don't mind in this case, though. If choosing the place had been up for a vote, Mira would've had mine as soon as she mentioned food poisoning.

Listening to their bickering, I wonder how interesting it must be to have a sibling. Or frustrating. I mean, what would it be like to have a younger sister? Especially one who's as reckless as Mira? I shudder at the thought.

"Table for three," Eugene tells the waiter when we enter the place.

"Ilona?" A deep voice says, and Mira winces. "Ya tebya ne uznal." Or at least that's what it sounds like. It's coming from a tall, well-built guy with a tattoo in the shape of an anchor on his muscular forearm.

Mira walks over to him, hugs him, and kisses him on the cheek. They start talking out of earshot from us. Eugene crosses his arms and eyes the guy suspiciously.

"Can we get a table as far away as possible from that man?" he asks the waiter.

"I can put you in the privacy of one of our tatami rooms," the waiter offers.

"Thank you," I say, and slip a twenty into his hand. "Please make it the furthest one."

Mira heads back to us. She puts a finger to her lips when her back is to the guy.

We are quiet until we get to the tatami room.

"I will not discuss it," Mira says when we sit down.

Eugene glares at her. She doesn't even blink, opening her menu and pointedly ignoring her brother.

"I thought I told you not to do that anymore," Eugene says in a hushed tone. "I thought I told you not to deal with thugs. You won't find him—but you will get yourself killed. Or worse."

"Ot-yebis' Eugene," Mira says, her face getting flushed. Whatever she just said, Eugene takes a breath and stops talking.

The waiter comes, asking what we want to drink. Mira orders hot sake, showing the waiter what must be a fake ID. I stick with green tea, as does Eugene.

I'm dying of curiosity. Did I mention it's one of my few weaknesses?

It feels risky, but I can't help myself. I phase into the Quiet and watch the frozen faces of Mira and Eugene carefully.

They don't seem to be in the Quiet with me. If what Eugene said is true, pulling them in requires explicitly touching them. That's good. I don't plan to do that.

I walk out of the little alcove room the waiter gave us and go through the restaurant, searching for the guy Mira spoke to when we first arrived. His table is empty, with only dirty plates and a check lying there. Apparently he was on his way out when we entered.

I walk through the frozen patrons to the door. Outside, I spot my target. He hasn't gone far.

First, I look in his pockets. Anton Gorshkov, his New York driver's license tells me. Along with his age, height, and address on Brighton Beach. That doesn't tell me much. But I now have a new trick I've been itching to try again—the whole Reading thing.

I touch his forehead. I do the meditation. I realize as it starts that the process is a little quicker now.

* * *

We watch Ilona—whom I, Darren, know as Mira—walking toward us. We don't know the men she's with. We barely recognize her without the tight dress and heels she's usually wearing.

"Anton, kakimi sud'bami?" she says to us. It should've sounded like gibberish to me, Darren, but I gleefully realize that I understand exactly what she said. The approximate meaning is: "I'm surprised to see you here, Anton." And I'm aware of the full, subtle meaning of her words, which doesn't translate to English. In general, I understand every thought that goes through Anton's head. Apparently language doesn't seem to matter when it comes to Reading, which makes a weird kind of sense.

We shrug and say, "What are you doing here?"

"Decided to grab a bite to eat," Ilona/Mira responds in Russian.

"Who are the wimps with you?" we say. Again, the translation is approximate. The word for 'wimps' has a more insulting connotation in the original Russian.

"Math geeks," she answers. "I consult with them on how to improve my game."

We have a flashback to playing cards with Ilona. She's good. One of the best. We try to look at her companions, but she blocks our way.

"They work exclusively with me," she says. Then, seeing our stubborn look, she adds, "Viktor introduced us."

We now lose any inclination to look at the math geeks. Not when Viktor is involved. People who cross that guy lose their heads. Literally. There was a rumor that Viktor tapped Ilona, and perhaps it's true. We really don't want anything to do with him.

"It was good seeing you. Maybe I'll see you at this weekend's big game?" she says.

"I doubt it," we say. "I first need to collect some

money."

I, Darren, try to go deeper.

Suddenly, it's late evening, and we're beating a guy in an alley. He's refused to get protection. Who does he think he is? Every Russian-owned business in this neighborhood pays protection money to Anton. Our fist aches, but we keep on pounding. No pain, no gain, we joke to ourselves. I, Darren, am horrified, but go deeper still.

Now we're sitting at a card game. We have a gambling 'hard on,' as we call it. I, Darren, can't believe my eyes.

In this dark room, filled with cigarette smoke and sketchy-looking characters whom we—Anton and me—find scary, there is Ilona. Or Mira, as I, Darren, remind myself.

She's wearing a tight dress, showing off her impressive cleavage.

We look at our cards. We have two pairs. We are golden. We bet to the limit.

She drops out. *Can she read our 'tells'?* we wonder, impressed.

The game moves forward.

Ilona wins the next round, calling one guy's bluff. We had no clue the fucker was bluffing. She deserves her reputation as a card prodigy.

As far as we know, she's never been accused of cheating. But we wonder how such a young, pretty thing can be this good without something up her sleeve. Then we chuckle at the realization that, in fact, she has no sleeves. With that strappy little dress, there's no fucking way she can be hiding cards.

Maybe someone at the table is cheating, and she's the partner? If that's the case, we'll keep our mouth shut. These men are not the kind of people you can accuse of cheating and live.

After seeing the game through, I, Darren, have had enough.

* * *

I am out of Anton's head. The experience of being someone else, even a lowlife like him, is beyond words. I'm going to do this over and over, until I get sick of it—which is probably never going to happen. It's so cool.

Right now, though, instead of enjoying the novelty of this experience, I'm wondering about Mira's sanity. I recall reading something about underground gambling and links to organized crime in her file in Atlantic City, but seeing it through this degenerate's eyes really put things in perspective for me.

Mira is nuts to be doing this. Why is she doing it? A Reader like her has to have a safer way to make money. Does she need something else in the criminal society? Eugene dropped a few hints about her looking for something or someone, but I still don't get it. A green monster in me wonders if she finds these men appealing. Anton did think of some scary guy who maybe had her protected or something like that.

Whatever the answers, I will not find them anytime soon. I have no intention of letting Mira know I learned any of this.

If she knew I snooped like this, it would kill whatever little trust she has in me—if she has any, that is.

CHAPTER ELEVEN

I re-enter the restaurant and find my way back to our little room. Then I touch myself on the forehead.

I'm back in my body. The sounds return.

"I must admit I love these places," I say, making small talk to cover any weirdness in my demeanor. "It's like a little piece of Japan in the middle of Brooklyn. This one isn't as hardcore as some I've seen. At least we're allowed to keep our shoes on."

Mira and Eugene comment on how some places in Brooklyn are more like that. Some do make you take your shoes off, and their servers wear kimonos.

I breathe easier. I officially got away with the little bit of snooping.

We all examine the menus.

"So, Darren, how long can you stay in the Mind Dimension?" Mira says nonchalantly, resuming the conversation.

"Mira," Eugene says, reddening as he looks up at his sister. "That's not very polite."

"Why is that not polite?" I ask, surprised. "Isn't Mind Dimension what she calls the place you guys 'Split' into? The place I call the Quiet?"

"The Quiet? How cute," Mira says, making me wonder if sarcasm is just the way she normally talks.

"Yes, Darren, that's what she's talking about," Eugene says, still looking embarrassed. "But what you don't know—and what Mira wants to take advantage of—is that this question is very personal in Reader society."

"Well, we're not in Reader society," Mira counters. "We're outcasts, so anything goes."

"Why is it such a big deal?" I ask, looking from brother to sister.

"In the Reader society proper, it's like asking someone how much money he's worth, or the size of his penis," Eugene explains as Mira chuckles derisively. "The time she asked you about is the measure of our power. It determines Reading Depth, for example, which is how far you can see into your target's memories. It also determines how long you can keep someone else in there. I'm surprised you even ask this, Darren. It seems self-evident how important this time is, since even without knowing about Reading Depth, there's the simple matter of longer subjective life experience."

"Of what?" I almost choke on my green tea. "What do you mean 'longer subjective life experience'?"

"You have got to be kidding me," Mira says, downing a shot of her hot sake. "Don't you know anything? I feel educated all of a sudden, and this is coming from a high school dropout."

I don't even question the dropout comment. I'm still on the life experience thing.

"You don't age while in the Mind Dimension," Eugene says. "So the longer you can stay there, the more you can experience."

"You don't age?" I can't believe I didn't think of it myself. If you don't eat or sleep, why am I surprised that you don't age?

"No, there's no aging that anyone's ever noticed," Eugene says. "And some of the Enlightened, the most powerful among us, can and do spend a long time in there."

I just sit there trying to readjust my whole world, which is becoming a common occurrence today.

When the waiter comes back, I order my usual Japanese favorite on autopilot. Eugene and Mira order as well.

"It's not that strange, if you think about it," Mira says when the waiter is out of earshot. "Time stands still there, or seems to."

"We don't know that," Eugene says. "It could also be that we're not there in a real, physical sense. Only our minds, or more specifically, our consciousness."

Mira rolls her eyes at him, but my mind is blown. "I was always bored when I spent too much time in there. I only used it when I was under some time crunch," I tell them, realizing all the opportunities I missed so far. "If I had only known . . . Are you saying that with every book I read in the physical world, I was literally wasting my life away—since I could've done it in the Quiet and not aged by those hours?"

"Yes," Mira says unkindly. "You were wasting your life away, as you are wasting ours right now."

She uses sarcasm so much that I've already become accustomed to it. It barely registers now. I'm more caught up in thinking about all the times I wasted hours of my life and the many millions of things I could've done in the Quiet. If only I had known that it would add more time to my life—or rather, not take time away from it. All this time, I thought I was just taking shortcuts.

"Well, I'm so glad I met you guys," I say finally. "Just knowing this one thing alone will literally change my life."

"Oh, and Reading wouldn't have?" Eugene winks.

I grin at him. "For that too, I'm forever in your debt and all that."

"Why don't you repay that debt a little by answering my question," Mira says, looking at me.

"Will you tell me yours if I tell you mine?" I joke.

"See how quickly his gratitude dissipates and turns into the usual tit for tat?" Mira says snarkily to Eugene.

I'm so flabbergasted by all the revelations that it barely registers that Mira just made a joke about tits.

"It's a deal," Eugene says, answering for his sister.

We pause our conversation when our food arrives. Eugene is served a three-roll special, Mira has a sushi bento box, and I have my sashimi deluxe. I'm a big fan of sushi—to me, it's like an edible work of art.

Returning to our discussion of how long I can stay in the Quiet, I say, "I can't give you an exact amount of time." Grabbing a piece of fatty salmon with my chopsticks, I explain, "As I said, I eventually get bored and phase out."

"But what's the longest you've ever been inside?" Eugene asks, adding a huge wad of wasabi into his tiny soy sauce bowl.

"A couple of days," I say. "I never really kept track of time."

Mira and Eugene exchange strange looks.

"You don't fall out of the Mind Dimension for a couple of days?" Mira says.

"What do you mean 'fall out'? I get bored and touch my skin to phase out. Is that what you mean?"

They exchange those looks again.

"No, Darren, she means fall out," Eugene says, looking at me like I'm some exotic animal. "When we reach our limit to being in that mode, what you call the Quiet, we involuntarily re-enter our bodies. For me, that happens after about fifteen minutes, which is considered pretty standard."

"I'm slightly above average for Readers, and practically a prodigy for a half-blood," Mira says, echoing his stare. "And my max time is a half hour. So you must see how this sounds to us. You're saying you can stay there for two entire days—or even longer, since you've never been pushed out."

"Right," I say, looking at them. "I never realized that was anything abnormal—well, more abnormal than going into the Quiet in the first place."

Eugene looks fascinated. "That would mean your mother had to have been extremely powerful. Almost at the Enlightened level, if you've never been forced out thus far."

"But if you get forced out, can't you just go right back in?" I say, confused.

"Are you messing with us?" Mira's eyes narrow.

"I think he really doesn't know," Eugene says. "Darren, once we get pushed out, we can't go right back in. The recuperation time is proportional to how long we can stay there, though it's not directly related. There's a strong inverse correlation between short recovery times and longer times in the Mind Dimension. So the elites get the best of both worlds: a short recovery time and a long time inside. How it all works in the brain is actually my area of research."

"Eugene, please, not the neuroscience again," Mira says with exasperation before turning her attention to me. "Darren, if you truly don't know about recuperation time, then your power must be off the charts. Only I didn't think a half-blood could have that much power." The look she gives me now is unsettling. I think I prefer disdain. This look is calculating, as though she's sizing me up.

"You have to let me study you," Eugene tells me. "So we can figure out some answers."

"Sure, I guess. It's the least I can do," I say uncertainly.

"Great. How about tomorrow?" Eugene looks excited.

"Hmm. Maybe the day after?"

He smiles. "Let me guess, you're going to spend a whole day going around Reading people's minds, aren't you?"

"Good guess," I say, smiling back.

"Okay. Thursday then," he says. He looks ecstatic at the prospect of putting more electrodes to my head.

"So, I can't Read another Reader's mind?" I ask as I eat a piece of pickled ginger. This is a question that's been bothering me for a bit.

"No. But I bet you wish you could," Mira answers, downing the last of her sushi.

"It's only possible to do that to someone before they learn to Split for the first time, when they're children," Eugene explains. "Once people have experienced the Split, they simply get pulled into your Mind Dimension with you if you try to Read them."

"And if you and I manage to Split at the same time?" I ask. "Would we see each other in there?"

"Now you're getting into very specific and rare

stuff," Eugene says. "It's almost impossible to time it that perfectly. Dad and I managed it only once. Even if you did, you'll find that, no, you see the world still, as usual, but you don't encounter each other. The only way to have a joint experience is to pull someone in. If either of you touches the other, the other will get pulled in. Once that happens, you'll be using up the time of the person whose Mind Dimension you're in."

"Using up the time?" I ask, finishing the last bit of my sashimi. This was amazing fish, I realize belatedly.

"As you bring people with you, your time is shared with them. If I pull you in, together we would stay in my Mind Dimension for about seven or eight minutes—about half of my fifteen-minute total. Similarly, how deep you go into someone's memories is half your total time."

The Reading Depth thing gives me an idea. If what Eugene says is right, then I think I have a better gauge of my 'power' based on my Reading of Eugene and Mira's neighbor, Brad. That sci-fi flick that he and Mira watched at the theater left the big screen at least six months ago—which means that I can spend at least a year in the Quiet.

As blown away as I am by this realization, something prevents me from sharing this information with my new friends. They looked awestruck at the mention of two days. What would they say to a year? And how do I reconcile this and being a half-blood? How powerful is Sara, to give birth to someone like me?

"What's the maximum power a Reader can have?" I ask instead.

"That's something even people who are part of the regular Reader society probably don't know," Mira says. "And even if they did, they wouldn't share that information with us."

"There are legends, though," Eugene says. "Legends of the Enlightened, who were wise well beyond their years. It was as though they'd led whole extra lifetimes. Of course, some of these stories seem more like mythology than history."

Myth or not, the stories sound fascinating. Before I get a chance to think about them, however, I'm interrupted by the waiter who brings our check. I insist on paying despite a few feeble complaints from Eugene. It's part of my thank you to them, I say.

When we exit the restaurant, I tell them, "I wish we could talk for hours on end, but there's something I have to do now."

"You could pull us into the Mind Dimension and chat away; this way you wouldn't be late for your appointment," Mira says, giving me a sly look.

"Mira." Eugene sounds chiding again.

She must be breaking another Reader social rule I'm not aware of. Using someone for time, perhaps? It doesn't matter. I wouldn't mind doing what she's asking if I wasn't dying of curiosity. "It's not about being late," I explain apologetically. "It's about asking my mom some serious questions."

"Oh, in that case, good luck," Mira says, her voice sympathetic for the first time.

"Thanks. Do you guys know where I can rent a car around here?"

Going to Staten Island from Brooklyn, or from anywhere for that matter, is best to do by car. There's a ferry from downtown, but no thanks. That requires taking a bus afterwards. And the ferry is unpleasant enough by itself.

Though Eugene and Mira don't know about rentals, my trusty phone does. According to it, there's a rental place a couple of blocks away. Since it's on the way to their apartment, I get an armed escort to the place—Mira with her gun. I'm grateful for that, as I'm still not a fan of their neighborhood. On our short walk, we talk some more about Readers. Despite Mira's complaints, Eugene starts telling me about his research.

It sounds like he's trying to find neural correlates that accompany what Readers do. That discovery might lead to knowing how the process works. He thinks he knows approximately what goes on, all the way up to the Split. After that moment, things get complicated because technology is finicky in the Quiet, and the instruments remaining in the real world don't register anything—proving that no time passes in the real world after we phase in.

I only half-listen. It all sounds fascinating, but in my mind, I'm already having a conversation with Sara.

When we reach the rental place, I enter both Eugene's and Mira's phone numbers into my phone, and they get mine. We say our goodbyes. Eugene shakes my hand enthusiastically. "It was great to meet you, Darren."

"Likewise," I say. "It was great meeting you both."

Mira walks up to me, and gives me a hug and a kiss on the cheek. I stand there wondering if that means she likes me, or if it's just a Russian thing. Whatever the reason for her actions, it was nice. I can still smell a hint of her perfume.

When they begin to head back, I turn to enter the car rental place. Before I do, I'm pulled into the Quiet again.

It's Mira.

"Darren," she says, "I want to thank you. I

haven't seen Eugene this happy, this animated, for a long time."

"Don't mention it. I like your brother," I say, smiling. "I'm glad I had that effect on him."

"I also wanted to say that, as he *is* my brother, I, above all, don't want to see him hurt."

"That makes sense." I nod agreeably.

"Then we have an understanding," she says evenly. "If this whole thing is a lie, I'll be extremely upset." Her eyes gleam darkly. "To put it in other words, if you hurt my brother in any way, I will kill you."

She turns around and walks to her frozen body, which is standing a few feet away.

I don't get a hug this time around.

CHAPTER TWELVE

I'm driving the piece-of-shit car I picked up at the rental place. They didn't have anything nice, but at least this thing has Bluetooth, so I'm listening to Enigma's "T.N.T. for the Brain" from my phone on the car speakers. I raise the volume to the max.

In a confused stupor, trying to digest everything I've learned today, I follow my phone's GPS directions. I know I need the Belt Parkway and the Verrazano Bridge after that, but once I get on Staten Island, I typically get lost—usually only a few blocks from where my moms live.

I called ahead to make sure they were home, but mentioned nothing of what I want to discuss. I plan to ambush them with my questions. They deserve it. I love them dearly, but I've never been angrier with them than I am now—not even during my rebellious mid-teen years. I'm especially mad at Sara.

Alternative lifestyle aside, Sara and Lucy are living, breathing stereotypes of two similar, yet different, kinds of moms.

Take Sara, for instance. She's a Jewish mom to the core. Never mind that she's the most secular person you'll ever meet. Never mind that she married a non-Jew, which isn't kosher. She still regularly hints—and sometimes outright says—that since I've finished my degree from a good school (of course), I should meet a nice girl (meaning a Jewish girl) and settle down. At twenty-one. Right. And she has all the usual guilt-trip skills down to a T. For example, if I don't call for a couple of days, I get the whole 'you don't need to trouble yourself to call your own mother; it's not like I'm in any way important,' et cetera, et cetera. And then there's the weird stuff, like if I'm out late and make the mistake of mentioning it to her, she'll want me to text her when I get home. *Yeah.* Never mind that on other nights—when I don't talk to her—I might not come home at all, and she's fine with my lack of texting.

Lucy is no better. Well, in truth, Lucy is better now. She only expects a call from me once a week, not daily. But when I was growing up, she was worse than Sara. She must've read that book about being a Tiger Mom and tried to apply it literally, with probably the worst possible subject—me. In hindsight, I think I had ADHD when I was a kid. When it came to the violin lessons she tried to force me to take, I 'accidentally' broke a dozen of the stupid instruments to test her resolve. When I broke the last one (over another student's head), I was expelled, and that did it for musical initiatives. Then there were the ballet lessons. I was kicked out for beating up a girl, which was not true. I knew from a very early age that you don't hit girls. Another girl pushed the victim, but I, because of my reputation in the class, took the rap. Lucy also wanted me to learn her native Mandarin. I don't care if I mastered a little bit from her when I was a baby, or that I can string together a few sentences even to this day; that was just not going to happen. If I'd studied Mandarin for her, I would've had to take Yiddish lessons for Sarah, too. Oy vey.

So, finishing school early and going to Harvard was partially an attempt to make my mothers happy, but even more so a means to get away from their overzealous parenting techniques and experience some freedom in Boston. Not to mention that finishing college allowed me to get a job and my own place as soon as possible. Ever since I gained some distance, my love for my family has deepened greatly.

As I pull into their driveway, I see three cars outside. I recognize the extra car as Uncle Kyle's old Crown Victoria.

Great, he's here. That's the last thing I need.

"Hi Mom," I say when Sara opens the door. I've never really seen much of myself in her, which makes me wonder that much more now about who my father might have been. We both have blue eyes, and I could've inherited her height, I guess. At five foot seven, she's tall for a woman. She seems particularly tall when, like now, she's standing next to my other mom. Lucy is barely above five feet tall, but don't let her size deceive you. She's tough. Plus, she has a gun—and knows how to use it.

"Hi sweetie," Sara says, beaming at me.

"Hi Mom," I say again, this time looking at Lucy.

"Hi Kitten," Lucy says.

Hmm. Are they trying to embarrass me in front of Uncle Kyle?

"Hey Kyle," I say with a lot less enthusiasm as I walk in.

He smiles at me, a rarity from him, and we shake hands.

I have mixed feelings when it comes to Kyle. Even though I mentally call him uncle, he's not my blood relative. Sara was an only child. He's a detective who works with Lucy. As former partners, I guess he and Lucy are close—a camaraderie I don't pretend to understand, having never put my life in danger the way they have.

I imagine my moms decided to ask Kyle to come around when I was growing up so I'd have a male role model in my life. However, their choice for the task couldn't have been worse. As far back as I can remember, I've butted heads with Kyle. Pick an issue, and we're likely to be on opposite sides of it. Doctor-assisted suicide, the death penalty, cloning humans, you name it, and you can be sure we've had a shouting match over it. I like to think of myself as a free thinker, while Kyle clings to what was digested and fed to him by some form of authority, never stopping to question anything.

The biggest mystery to me is actually why someone so traditional even accepts my moms' relationship. My theory is that he has a mental disconnect. I imagine he tells himself that despite their marriage, they're just best friends who live together.

I also think he has a rather tragic crush on Lucy. He would call it brotherly love, but I've always been skeptical. Especially given his very professional, cold attitude toward Sara, a woman he's known for over twenty years. An attitude that was chilly all along, but grew downright frigid after the huge fight they had when he decided to discipline me with a belt when I was nine. I was clever enough to scream and cry like a banshee, and predictably, Sara had a major fit. She actually threw a vase in his face. I think he had to get stitches. After that, he only used words to discipline me, and his interactions with Sara became even more aloof.

Having said all that, after I stopped needing to deal with Kyle regularly, I began to feel more fondness for the bastard. I know he usually means well. He's the closest thing to a father figure I have, and he did come around a lot, generally with good intentions. He told me cool stories about back in the day when he and Lucy kicked ass and took names— stories Lucy never chose to share, for some reason. And I wouldn't be half as good a debater now if not for all that arguing with him. For better or for worse, he played a role in the person I've become, and that's an honor usually reserved for people you consider close.

"How's work?" Kyle asks. "Are we due for another financial meltdown anytime soon?"

Kyle isn't a fan of anyone in the financial

industry. I can forgive that; few people are fans of them. Or should I say of us? Also, only a tiny portion of the population understands the difference between bankers and hedge fund analysts, or can tell any financial professional from another.

"Work is great," I respond. "I'm researching a biotech company that's going to use magnetic waves to manipulate human brains for therapy."

Lucy narrows her eyes at me. She knows I'm trying to start an argument again. But I have to hand it to Kyle: this time, he doesn't take the bait. Usually he would go into some Luddite bullshit about how frightening and unnatural what I just said sounds, how dangerous it is to mess with people's brains like that. But no, he doesn't say anything of the sort.

"I'm glad you're making a name for yourself at that company," he says instead. Is that an olive branch? "I was just on my way out, but I'll see you at Lucy's birthday party in a few weeks."

"Sure, Kyle," I say. "See you then."

He walks out, and Lucy walks out with him. He probably came to get her advice on a case. He does that to this day, despite not having been her partner for decades.

"When will you grow up?" Sara chides, smiling. "Why must you always push people's buttons?"

"Oh, that's rich, you defending Kyle." I roll my

eyes.

"He's a good man," she says, shrugging.

"Whatever," I say, dismissing the subject with a single word. The last thing I'm interested in right now is an argument about Kyle. "We need to talk. You should actually sit down for this."

Alarm is written all over Sara's face. I'm not sure what she imagines I'm going to say, but she has a tendency to expect the worst.

"Should we wait for your mother?" she says. They both say that in reference to the other, and it's always funny to me. *Your mother.*

"Probably. It's nothing bad. I just have some important questions," I say. Despite everything, I feel guilty that I've worried her.

I notice that she pales at the mention of important questions.

"Are you hungry?" she asks, looking me up and down with concern. *Please, not the too-thin talk again.* If it weren't for Lucy intervening, my own lack of appetite, and my stubbornness, I would be the chubbiest son Sara could possibly raise. And the fatter I'd get, the happier Sara would be as a mom. She would be able to show me around and say 'see how fat he is, that's how much I love him.' I know she got that 'feeding is caring' attitude from Grandma, who wouldn't rest until you were as big as a house.

The fact that Sara doesn't pursue the food topic now shows me how concerned she is. Is it some kind of guilt thing? Does she suspect what I'm about to ask?

"No, thanks, Mom. I just had some sushi," I say. "But I would love some coffee."

"Did you go out partying all night?" She appears even more worried now. "You look exhausted."

"I didn't sleep well last night, but I'm okay, Mom."

She shakes her head and goes into the kitchen. I follow. Their house is still unfamiliar. I preferred the cramped Manhattan apartment where I grew up, but my moms decided a few years back that it was time for the suburbs and home ownership. At least they have some of the same familiar furniture I remember from childhood, like the chair I'm now sitting in. And the heavy round kitchen table. And the cup, red with polka dots, that she hands to me. My cup.

"I smell coffee," Lucy says, coming back.

"I made you a cup, too," Sara says.

"You read my mind," Lucy responds, smiling.

I decide I'm not going to get a better segue than that. Is it literally true? Can Sara Read Lucy's mind?

"Mom," I say to Sara. "Is there something

important you want to tell me about my heritage?"

I look at them both. They look shell-shocked.

"How did you figure it out?" Lucy asks, staring at me.

"I'm so sorry," Sara says guiltily.

The vehemence of their reaction confuses me, considering my relatively innocuous question. I haven't even gotten to the heavy stuff yet. But it seems like I'm onto something, so I just say nothing and try to look as blank as I can, since I'm not sure what we're talking about. I sense we're not exactly on the same page.

"We always meant to tell you," Sara continues, tears forming in her eyes. "But it never seemed like a good time."

"For the longest time, until you were in your mid-teens, we couldn't discuss it at all. Even among ourselves," Lucy adds. She isn't tearing up, but I can tell she's distraught. "We even tried reading books about it. But the books recommend saying it as early as possible, which we didn't do . . ."

"Saying what?" I ask, my voice rising. I'm reasonably certain I'm about to find out something other than what I came here to verify, since I'm not aware of any books about Reading.

Sara blinks at me through her tears. "I thought

you knew . . . Isn't that what you want to talk about? I thought you used some modern DNA test to figure it out."

A wave of panic washes over me. I try not to phase. I want to hear this.

"I want to know what you're talking about," I say. "Right now."

I look at them in turn. Daring them to try to wiggle out of it. They know they have to spill the beans now.

"You were adopted, Darren," Lucy says quietly, looking at me.

"Yes," Sara whispers. "I'm not your biological mother." She starts to cry, something I've hated since I was a little kid. There's something wrong, weirdly scary, about seeing your mom cry. Except—and the full enormity of it dawns on me—she's not my birth mom.

She never has been.

CHAPTER THIRTEEN

How would anyone react in my shoes?

I don't know if it's seeing my moms so upset or the news itself, but I can't take the flood of emotion for long. I phase into the Quiet. Once the world around me is still, I pick up the coffee cup and throw it across the room. It shatters against the TV, coffee spilling everywhere. I get up, grab the empty chair next to the one where my frozen self is sitting, and hurl it across the room after the cup, yelling as loudly as I can. I stop myself from breaking more stuff, though; even though I know it will go back to normal after I phase out, it still feels like vandalism.

Then I take a couple of deep breaths, trying to

pull myself together.

This explains things—things that Eugene and Mira told me about. Sara didn't lie to me. She never had my ability. She reacted to my descriptions of the Quiet as a normal person would. I should probably feel relieved. I feel anything but.

Why would they not tell me? After all, it's not like we haven't had conversations about being adopted. We had them all the time. Sort of. We talked about how Lucy didn't give birth to me, but loves me just as much as Sara who, allegedly, did. This would've been just more of the same.

I take more deep breaths. I sit on the floor and perform the meditation I have used four times already today.

I begin to feel better—well enough to continue talking, at least. I look at the shocked expression on my frozen face. I reach out and touch myself on the elbow. The gesture is intended to comfort the frozen me, which, once I do it, seems silly. The touch brings me out of the Quiet.

I take a deep breath more demonstratively in the real world. "If you're not my biological mother," I manage to say, "then who is?"

"Your parents' names were Mark and Margret," Lucy says. To my shock, she's crying too— something I've almost never seen her do. A knot ties itself in the pit of my stomach as she continues, "Your uncle might've told you stories about Mark."

I'm almost ready to phase into the Quiet again. She said 'were.' I know what that means. And I have heard of Mark. He was the daredevil partner who worked with Lucy and Kyle.

"Tell me everything," I say through clenched teeth. I'm trying my best not to say something I'll regret later.

"Before you were born, we really did go to Israel, as we always told you," Sara begins, her voice shaking. "It's just that what happened there was different from what you know. Our friends Mark and Margret approached us with a crazy story, and an even crazier request."

She stops, looking at Lucy pleadingly.

"They said someone was out to kill them," says Lucy in a more even voice. "They said Margret was pregnant, and they wanted us to raise the child. To pretend it was our own." She gets calmer as she tells this, her tears stopping. "We always wanted a child. It seemed like a dream come true. They were the ones who came up with the whole sperm bank story. They said the danger they were in could spill into your life if anyone ever found out about the arrangement. I know it sounds like I'm making excuses for not telling you, but when they got killed, just as they moved back to New York to be near you . . ."

"Lucy and Mark were close," Sara jumps in, wiping away the moisture on her face. "Back then, they worked in the organized crime division together. Lucy and I just assumed the unit where they all worked had something to do with why Mark was killed, which is why I begged your mother to switch to another division." She looks at Lucy again, silently urging her to continue with the story.

"I investigated their deaths," Lucy says. "But I still, to this day, have no idea who killed them and why. The killer left no clues. The crime scene was the most thoroughly investigated one in my career—and nothing. All I know is that Margret was shot in the back in her own kitchen, and it looked like Mark was killed a few seconds later when he tried to attack the person who shot her. There were no signs of a break-in."

My mind's gone numb. How am I supposed to feel about something like this happening to the biological parents I never knew existed? Or about them giving me to their friends to raise, even though they knew they'd be putting Sara and Lucy in danger?

I can't take it anymore, so I phase into the Quiet again.

Once everything is still, I walk up to Sara, whose face is frozen in concern. I still love her, just as much as I did on my way here. This changes nothing. I've always loved Lucy the same as Sara, despite knowing we're not related by blood. As far as I can tell, this is no different.

I put my hand on Sara's forearm and try to get into the state of Coherence, as Eugene called it. I'm so worked up that it's much more difficult this time. I don't know how long it takes before I'm in Sara's memories.

* * *

We're excited Darren is going to visit.

I, Darren, feel ashamed somehow at the intensity of Sara's enthusiasm. If it makes her so happy, I should probably visit more often.

We're devastated at having the dreaded adoption conversation with Darren, after all these years. Our own little family secret. Before I, Darren, am naturally pushed out by getting to the present moment in Sara's memories, I decide to go deeper. Picturing being lighter, trying to focus, I fall further in.

We're watching Darren pack for Harvard. We're

beyond anxious. I, Darren, realize that I am not far enough and focus on going deeper.

We're on a date with Lucy. She's the coolest girl we have ever met. I, Darren, realize how creepy this thing I am doing can get, but I also know that I can't stop. I overshot my target memory mark and need to go back out of this depth, or in other words, fast-forward the memories. I, Darren, do what I tried before when I wanted to get deeper into someone's mind, only in reverse: I picture myself heavier. It works.

We've been obsessing about Israel for months. Our heritage must call us, as our mom Rose said. I, Darren, realize that Rose is Grandma and that I am close—and I jump a bit further this time by picturing myself heavier again.

We're in Israel. It's awesome. Even Lucy's initial grumpy 'there are almost no other Asians here' attitude gets turned around after spending a day at the beach.

We look around the beach. The view is breathtaking. I, Darren, make a note to visit this place someday.

"Hi guys," says a familiar male voice.

We're shocked to see the M&Ms, Mark and Margret, approach our chairs. So is Lucy, we bet. What could they possibly be doing here, in Israel?

The last thing anyone expects when going overseas is to meet friends from New York.

I, Darren, see them, and Sara's surprise pales next to mine. It's not like they look exactly like me, Darren. But it's almost like some Photoshop genius took their facial features, mixed them up, added a few random ones, and got the familiar face that, I, Darren, see every day in the mirror.

"What are you doing here?" Lucy asks, looking concerned.

"We need to talk," Mark says. "But not here."

I, Darren, picture feeling heavy again, so I can jump forward a little more.

We're listening to the M&Ms' crazy tale.

"Who's after you? If you don't tell me, how am I supposed to help?" Lucy says in frustration after they're done. We feel the same way. We can't believe our friends are springing this on us and telling us next to nothing.

"Don't ask me that, Lucy. If I told you, I'd put you and, by extension, the unborn child in danger," Mark says. I, Darren, realize that his voice is deep, a lot like the voice I hear on my voicemail. My voice.

"But what about you?" we say, looking at Margret. "How will you be able to go through with this?"

Margret, who has been very quiet through this conversation, begins crying, and we feel like a jerk.

"Margie and I are both willing to do whatever it takes to make sure our child lives," Mark says for her. "Regardless of how much it hurts us to distance ourselves this way."

"So you won't come back to New York?" Lucy asks. That's our girl, always the detective, trying to put every piece together.

He shakes his head. "My resignation is already prepared. We'll stay in Israel until the baby is born, then come back to New York for the first year of the baby's life to help you guys, and then we'll move to California. We hope you can come visit us in California once the baby is older. Tell her—or him—that we're old friends." Mark's voice breaks.

"But this makes no sense," Lucy says, echoing our thoughts. "If you're going to quit and move anyway, the child should be safe enough—"

"No," Mark says. "Moving barely mitigates the risk. The people who want us dead can reach us anywhere. Please don't interrogate me, Lucy. Just think how wonderful it would be to have a child. Weren't you guys always planning to adopt?"

"We couldn't think of better people to trust with this," Margret says. "Please, help us."

We think she's trying to convince herself of her

decision. We can't even imagine how she must be feeling.

"We'll pay for everything," Mark says, changing the subject.

We're in complete agreement with Lucy's objections to the money, but in the end, the M&Ms convince us to accept their extremely generous offer—money we didn't even know they had. We know what Mark's approximate salary range is, since he works with Lucy, and he can't be making that much more than she is. To someone with that salary, this kind of money is unheard of. Nor is it likely that Margret makes that much. We wonder if having so much money has something to do with the paranoid story of people coming after them.

I, Darren, however, don't think it's the money. Could it be the Pushers? After all, Pushers killed Mira and Eugene's family. Could they be behind killing mine? Learning more about Pushers becomes much more personal for me all of a sudden.

I, Darren, can't take any more of this unfolding tragedy. I might come back here someday, but I can't handle it right now. Still, like a masochist, I progress into the memories.

We're driving back from Margret and Mark's funeral. We haven't spoken most of the way. We have never seen Lucy this upset.

"Please talk to me, hon," we say, trying to break the heavy silence.

"I was the one who found the bodies," Lucy says, her voice unrecognizable. "And I did the most thorough sweep of the crime scene. And with all that, I have nothing. It's like a perfect, unsolvable crime from one of your detective stories. I can't take it. I owe it to Mark to find the fucker who did this . . ."

"Don't be so hard on yourself," we say. "You'll figure it out. If you can't, no one could."

"We should have moved," Lucy says.

She hits a weak spot—our own guilt. We wish we had told Mark and Margret not to come to New York for that first year, not if they were in that much danger. But we didn't tell them that. We could've offered to come to California for a year. Something. The biggest source of our guilt, though, is that we thought the M&Ms were crazy. We didn't delve deeper into their story because it led to the most miraculous result—Darren. But now that Mark and Margret are dead, they are vindicated. We don't think they were crazy anymore. We just feel horrible for doubting them and not preventing this disaster somehow.

I, Darren, officially can't take any more. I jump out of Sara's head.

* * *

I'm back in the Quiet, looking at Sara. Much of my anger has dissipated. How can I be angry after I just experienced how this woman feels about me? I feel a pang of guilt for having invaded my mother's privacy to get the truth, but it's over and done with now.

I walk toward myself and touch my elbow.

Though I'm out of the Quiet, Sara is still pretty much motionless, waiting for my reaction.

"I don't know what to say," I say truthfully.

"It's okay. It's a lot to process," Lucy says.

"You think?" I say unkindly, and immediately regret it when she winces.

"I'm sorry it took us so long to tell you," Sara says, looking guilty.

"Even today, you told me under duress," I say, unable to resist. I guess I still feel bitter about that— about being kept in the dark for so long.

"I guess that's true," Sara admits. "Like Lucy said, we had a hard time talking about this for years. Once you don't talk about something, it becomes this strange taboo. But if you didn't already know, what were you asking about before?" She gives me a puzzled look.

"Never mind that now," I say. No way am I ready

to spout some crazy talk about being part of a secret group of people who can freeze time and get into the minds of others. I was only going to bring that up when I thought Sara was a Reader herself. "The most important thing is that what you told me doesn't change anything for me."

I know from just Reading her mind that this is what she most wants to hear. I mean it, too. Yes, I'm mad and confused now, but I know with time what I just said will be one hundred percent true. It will be as though this adoption conversation never happened.

For those words, I'm rewarded by the expressions of relief on their faces.

"If you don't mind, I want to go home right now. I need to digest all this," I tell them. This is riskier. I know they would rather I stay and hang out. But I really am beyond exhaustion at this point.

"Sure," Sara says, but I can tell she's disappointed.

"We're here to answer any questions you might have," Lucy says. Her expression is harder to read.

Lucy is right. I might have questions later. But for now, I kiss and hug them before getting out of there as quickly as I can.

The drive to Tribeca happens as if in a dream. I only become cognizant of the actual mechanics of it when I start wondering where to park. Parking in the city is a huge pain, and is the reason I don't own a car. I opt for one of the paid parking lots, despite having to pay something outrageous for it tomorrow. Right now, I don't care. Anything to get home.

Once I get to my apartment, all I have the energy to do is eat and shower. After that, I fall asleep as soon as my head hits the pillow.

CHAPTER FOURTEEN

It's amazing what a good night's sleep can do for the psyche. As I'm eating my morning oatmeal, I see the events and revelations of the prior day in a brand-new light. Even the adoption thing seems like something I can deal with.

I try to put myself in my moms' shoes. Let's say my friend Bert told me a strange secret. Let's further suppose he asked me not to tell it to anyone, and then died. Surely that would count as sort of like someone's dying wish. And as such, it would undoubtedly be hard to reveal the secret in those circumstances. Could that be part of the reason for my moms' lack of communication?

Now that I'm more rested, I also realize another aspect of my new situation: I might have some family I've never met. Grandmothers and grandfathers I didn't know existed. Maybe uncles and cousins. All of these new family members are probably out there in the mysterious Reader community. It's too bad Eugene and Mira are not part of said community. If they were, I would have a way of getting introduced to other Readers. Maybe I'd even meet my extended family and learn more about my heritage.

Also, now that I'm not so stressed, knowledge of my newfound skills begins to excite me. I mean, think of the possibilities. It reminds me of middle school, when I first mastered the Quiet. I'd had a ton of fun sneaking into the girl's locker room unnoticed, reading my first girlfriend's diary, spying on hot older women . . . Now that I think about it, there was definitely a pattern to my early use of the Quiet.

All those things, however, pale in comparison to what Reading will let me do. It's almost best that I only learned about it now, when I'm more mature and better able to use this power responsibly.

The choice for my first destination is easy.

Finishing breakfast, I get dressed. I grab a Blu-ray disk that I should've returned ages ago and go to the third floor of my building.

I only went out with Jenny a few times. She's not in any way special among my ex-girlfriends, except for one thing—proximity. She lives in my building, which naturally makes her my first stop. Now what was I saying about being mature enough to handle this responsibly?

Stopping in front of her apartment door, I ring the doorbell.

Jenny opens the door. "Darren?" she says, looking at me. I'm tempted to deny it, to say that I'm not Darren, but figure she's not in the mood for jokes.

"I found this movie I borrowed from you," I say instead. "I wanted to give it back."

"Oh. Okay, I guess. I'm just surprised to see you." She doesn't look just surprised, though—she looks angry. Or at least a little unnerved. Figuring there's no time like the present, I phase into the Quiet.

There had been a slight buzzing in the hallways of my apartment building, something I only realize now because it's gone. It's interesting how we ignore constant noises like that. I started becoming more cognizant of just how much we don't register about our surroundings when I first began phasing into the Quiet. So much happens around us that our conscious mind misses.

I touch Jenny's forehead. Though I had been conflicted about touching women in the Quiet, I decide that this is different. Or that Reading is worth it. It's easy to convince myself to let go of certain principles when they get in the way of something I really want.

I try to get into Coherence. It's even easier this time. As soon as I'm in, I do the lightness bit in order to jump deeper into her thoughts—otherwise all I'll see is her opening the door for me, which is boring.

* * *

We're at a club, making out with a girlfriend in order to get attention from the guys. Though this is not where I, Darren, intended to end up, I'm content to stay for a little while. I try to absorb every moment. We dance and grind with Judy, but it's all just for fun, a way to get attention. Eventually I, Darren, lose interest and try to go deeper.

We're getting ready to meet with Darren again. We're a little sad about our relationship with him. He used to be so hot—until he paid attention to us. At that point, his appeal dropped drastically. Why does that always happen to us?

No, we have to stop being our own worst critic. It could be Darren who's the problem, not us. When we saw him at that party in the penthouse, he seemed so confident and cocky, exactly what turns us on. But then he didn't ask us to go to his place that night, coming up with some lame coffee date instead. That's on him. Unless of course we start worrying about being a slut. We wish one day the inner critic would just shut the fuck up.

We pick the outfit for this evening very carefully. The new bra and panties should go a long way. I, Darren, think I recognize what day this is, so I jump further, to the part of her life I actually came here to witness.

Darren is standing without his shirt in our bedroom. He's in great shape. We hope we turn him on. As things progress, we worry a lot less about anything, instead focusing on what we're feeling as we give in to the purely physical part of ourselves.

When the experience is over, I, Darren, jump out.

* * *

I'm back in the Quiet. Okay, yeah. I wanted to experience what sex is like for a girl. And what better way to do so than to find out what it would be like to have sex with *me*? Not to mention, I'm not entirely sure how I'd feel about experiencing sex as a girl with a guy who's not me. There's no way I'm sharing this with my therapist. She'd have a field day with it.

Both Coherence and moving about in people's memories are getting easier for me already. This reminds me of when I first discovered being able to go into the Quiet.

Skills improve with experience. With the first few trips into the Quiet, it took being near death to activate the strange experience. A fall from a bike was only the first. There was also a fall off a roof into a sandbox, and a bunch of other stunts culminating in the time I fell into that manhole. Crazy, right? Who falls into a manhole? According to my moms, their childhood nickname for me was Taz, after the Tasmanian Devil from the cartoons. That's how much trouble I used to get into. But at least it gave me practice when it came to near-death experiences.

Then it started happening under less dire circumstances, like the time I got into a fight with our school bully, John. I still hate that guy. I momentarily contemplate finding him, Reading his mind, and messing with him. I decide against it for now. I would need to locate the prick, and that's too much of a bother at the moment.

Eventually, getting into the Quiet would happen when I did something as insignificant as watch a good horror movie. Progressively I got to where I am today, where any slight worry or nervousness can be harnessed for phasing in. I wonder what the path was like for Eugene and Mira. I'll have to remember to ask them.

Thinking of those two makes me wonder if I should stop messing around and go see them. No, I decide. Not yet. Not until I have some more Reading fun.

I look at Jenny. She's clutching the door, like she wants to close it as soon as possible. I feel a pang of guilt, and I phase out.

"Sorry if I intruded," I say. "I guess I should've left this by the door. I just figured, since we agreed to stay friends, it would be a good idea to bring this to you."

"Yeah, sure," she says. It doesn't take Reading to know she didn't actually want us to be friends when she said that. "It was nice of you to bring this back, and I'm glad you didn't just leave it by the door like some stranger."

"Okay, thanks. Sorry I bugged you. I'll see you around," I say. It's awkward, but I don't regret this. Jenny looks like she knows she's missing something, but since I'm sure there's no way she'll ever guess what just happened, I don't worry about it.

The door closes, and I'm ready for a drive around the city.

On a whim, I decide to go to the gym. There are plenty of people I can Read there. Plus, it would be nice to get a workout. I exercise mostly out of vanity, but at the same time, I do like to hear how good exercise is for your mind as well as your body. More bang for the buck.

Instead of my usual Tribeca location, I go to the Wall Street branch—I have a car, after all, so I figure I may as well use it. The Wall Street gym is classier.

By the time I get there, which isn't far, I curse the car idea. I would have gotten here much faster on foot, considering the traffic and the time it takes to find a parking spot. That's Manhattan for you. It's got some minuses.

I walk through the big revolving glass doors. This gym in general, and this location specifically, is very high end. Its membership price is ridiculous, but hey, I can afford it. It's nice and clean, which is a huge bonus for me. I might be a little OCD when it comes to cleanliness.

I wonder if it would make sense to exercise in the Quiet anymore. I used to do it on occasion when I was in a rush, but that was before I knew you don't age in there. Now that I know about the aging thing, it seems logical that muscles wouldn't grow bigger from any exercise performed in the Quiet. And growing muscles is really the only reason I do this.

Still, I'm not one hundred percent sure that it would be useless to exercise in the Quiet in general.

Certainly some skills stay with you. Just the other week, when I was convinced to play my first game of golf, I practiced in the Quiet so my game would be more impressive to my coworkers. The practice definitely helped, meaning some kind of muscle memory was retained. Another question for Eugene, I guess.

For now, I opt for a real-world workout.

I'm doing chest presses when I see a familiar face. We have a lot of celebrities at this gym, so I try to recall who this is. Then it hits me. Can that really be who I think it is? It's possible—his bank's headquarters are near here. If he did go to a gym open to the public, this would be the one he'd go to.

To make sure I'm right, I approach him.

"Excuse me, can you please spot me?" I ask, pointing at the bench I'm using.

"Sure," he says. "Do you need a lift?"

"I got it," I say, and I do. That's him. Jason Spades, the CEO. The man is a hero to us at the fund. His is the only bank that weathered the shit storm that befell most others—and he got a lot of the credit for it. From what I heard, his fame is well deserved.

"Thanks," I tell him when I'm done with my set.

He walks away, and on a whim, I phase into the Quiet. It's particularly easy in the gym—the heart is already racing, which to the brain must not be far from being frightened or otherwise excited.

It's very odd to see people holding heavy weights suspended in midair, though. It seems like their hands should fail any second.

I walk up to Jason Spades and touch his temple. It's time to flex my Reading muscles some more. I have to work on the meditation to get into the Coherence state for a moment. Next, I picture myself light as a feather. I'm hoping to enter his mind further than what seems to happen by default.

* * *

"Go to the gym today, take a day off, and do some gardening. You can't beat yourself up like this," our wife tells us at the breakfast table. "This kind of stress will give you a heart attack."

"You don't understand, babe. It's going to be the worst quarter results in the company history. Back in the day, CEOs jumped out of windows over this sort of thing," we say. We are grateful for her support, but we can't help feeling that she just doesn't get it. The enormity of it. Everything we've worked for is going to be ruined. No weekends, no vacations, endless sleepless nights—all for nothing.

We also think about the other thing, the thing we haven't even mentioned to her. How a trader was taking unauthorized risks and lost a big chunk of the bank's money. We're going to be held responsible by the investors for that, too. Combined with the quarter results, we'll look like an idiot—just like the rest of the bank CEOs. This is not the legacy we'd been hoping for.

I, Darren, decide I've had enough and jump out.

* * *

I'm speechless, torn between empathy and glee.

I do feel bad for Jason. It's painful to see legendary people like that fall. His disappointment is intense. His wife is getting him through it, though, and that's encouraging. Maybe there is something to the whole marriage thing after all. And he's probably wrong about his wife—I bet she understands what's about to come down. She probably just knows the right things to say to her husband. On a slightly more positive side, I'm glad he wasn't contemplating something insane, like blowing his brains out. I don't know what I'd do in that case. Would I try to stop him? Probably I would, though how to start that conversation without seeming like a lunatic is beyond me.

Anyway, I can't dwell on these depressing thoughts. Not when Jason's tragedy can be my get-rich-ridiculously-quick scheme.

I phase out, and on an impulse, I take out my phone. Did I mention I love smartphones? Anyway, I bring up my trading app. The bank's stock is the highest it's been in the past four years. Clearly nobody has any idea what's about to happen.

I have to act. I check on the price of put options. Those are basically contracts with someone assuring you they'll buy from you at an agreed-upon price within a given time period. It turns out that an option to sell at a lower price than where the stock is right now is dirt-cheap. That's because put options are like insurance, and in this case, people are betting the price will be steady or higher. I have thirty-two thousand dollars in cash in my trading account, and I use it all to buy the put options.

With some very conservative assumptions, if the stock drops even ten percent, I'll still be able to make a lot, either by selling the options or exercising them. If the stock completely tanks, like that of the 'too big to fail' banks during the crisis, I might end up making a cool million from the money I just invested. And, of course, I'll invest more of my money when I'm near a computer. There's only so much you can do on the phone. I think I might even put all of my savings into this, though I have to be careful. The SEC might wonder about me if I go overboard. Also, what if I Read someone else and get an even better tip? My money would be locked up for a few weeks. Though, I have to admit, it's hard to picture a better scenario.

And regarding the SEC, I wish I knew at what point someone shows up on their radar. Not that they'd have anything on me, even if they noticed my activity. They work on proof, unlike the casinos— proof like phone conversations or email records. Things they would not have in my case. Still, I don't want the bother of an investigation.

I can't believe Mira makes her money playing cards with criminals. This way is so much easier. I really hope she doesn't do it for money. If I find out that's the case, and offer Eugene and her some money, I wonder if they would accept. Somehow I think she might be too proud, but I ought to try. I'm feeling very generous right now. I've never had any trouble with money, even without the job at the fund, but now, with Reading, I see that I will quickly reach a new level of financial independence.

I'm so wired now, I have to go harder on myself during the rest of the workout. Lifting heavy weights seems to clear my mind. I'm not sure if that's a common experience or just me being weird. There's only one way to find out, so I Read a few minds to investigate. According to my informal gym-based study, other people also feel good after lifting weights. Good to know.

When I'm done with the gym and get in my car, I text Amy. She's an acquaintance from Harvard. That's another reason to go there, by the way—to make important connections that help you get jobs.

Networking is not why I want to meet with Amy today, however. I do it because she's crazy, in exactly the way I need.

She wants to do sushi, and after some back-and-forth, I give in. I guess I'll have sushi for the second day in a row. It's a good thing I like the stuff so much.

We meet at her favorite midtown place and catch up. She works at another fund, so it's easy to convince her this is just an impromptu networking session. Except I'm here for a different reason.

Amy is into extreme experiences of all sorts. In some ways, she's the opposite of me. For example, she's just bitten into Fugu sashimi. Fugu is that poisonous blowfish that the Japanese never allowed their emperor to eat. The fish contains tetrodotoxin, a neurotoxin fatal to humans and other creatures. If the chef messed up Amy's order, it could be deadly. Each fish has enough poison to kill around thirty people. And Amy's eating it like it's nothing. That's the sort of person she is. It's perfect for me, so I phase into the Quiet.

Amy is still, chopsticks carrying their potentially deadly load into her mouth. She isn't cringing or anything. I have to respect her for that.

I approach her and get into her mind, not bothering to rewind events.

* * *

We're chewing the Fugu. I, Amy, can't get enough of the stuff, while I, Darren, am severely disappointed. The flavor is much too subtle for me. It doesn't really taste like much of anything. Given the health risks, I would've expected this to taste like lobster multiplied by a hundred.

I go deeper.

We're flying in a plane. This is our first non-tandem jump, and we feel the adrenaline rush just getting on the plane. When it takes us to fifteen thousand feet, we get our first 'feargasm,' as we like to call it.

When we eventually make the jump, the feeling of free fall overwhelms us with its intensity. It's everything we thought it would be, and more.

Through it all, we don't forget the most important thing—and after sixty seconds of bliss that seem like a millisecond, we pull the cord to open the parachute.

We're already wondering what to do next. Maybe jump naked? Maybe under the influence of some substance?

The flight after the parachute opens gets boring, so I, Darren, seek something else.

We're snowboarding this time . . .

* * *

I get out of Amy's head eventually. Thanks to her, I'm able to cross off ninety percent of my bucket list. Through her eyes, I have surfed, bungee jumped, rock climbed, snowboarded, and even done BASE jumping with a wing suit.

I would never have done any of these things for real, particularly since yesterday I found out something that I'm still trying to wrap my head around: I can extend my subjective lifespan by just chilling in the Quiet. That means I have a lot more to lose than regular people.

I insist on paying for Amy's lunch. It's the least I can do to pay her back for the experiences I just gleaned through her eyes. I definitely got closer to understanding what drives her and other people like her to do these seemingly crazy things. Most of it was awesome—especially jumping out of that plane.

Of course, it wasn't awesome enough for me to risk my life. But now, thanks to Reading, I won't have to. I can just hang out with Amy again. I think I might be getting lunch with her more often now.

After I'm in the car again by myself, I, unbelievably, feel like I might've had enough Reading for today. I want to get together with my new Brooklyn friends a day early.

I text Eugene, and he excitedly invites me over.

Now the stupid car will finally come in handy.

CHAPTER FIFTEEN

I park in front of Eugene and Mira's building after an uneventful drive over. The spot is near a fire hydrant, but far enough away from it not to get a ticket. The nice thing about hydrant spots like this is that there's no one in front of the car. This makes parallel parking, a skill I haven't fully mastered, easier. No parking meters either, just a regular spot that's only a problem during Monday morning street cleanings. Impressive. I guess one nice perk of Brooklyn is being able to park like this on the street.

I make my way over to the building entrance. A friendly old lady holds the door for me. Apparently I don't look like a burglar to her, the way she just lets me walk right in. I'm glad, because this way I don't have to play with the intercom again.

Before the door closes behind me, I get that feeling again.

Someone's pulled me into the Quiet.

The door is frozen halfway between open and shut, the world is silent, and I'm standing next to frozen me and unfrozen Mira. I briefly wonder what part of my body she touched to get me to join her before I notice the wild look in her eyes and forget everything else.

"Mira, what's going on?"

"There isn't time," she says, running to the stairs. "Follow me."

I run after her, trying to make sense of it.

"They found me," she says over her shoulder. "They found us."

"Who found you?" I ask, finally catching up.

She doesn't answer; instead she stops dead in her tracks. There are men standing like statues on the staircase heading up to the first floor.

Finally coming out of whatever shock she's in, she goes through the pockets of a tall burly man wearing a leather jacket. Not finding whatever information she was looking for in his wallet, she touches his temple and appears to be concentrating in order to

Read.

When she's done, she takes a gun from the man's inner pocket and shoots him. The sound of the shot, even with a silencer on the gun, nearly deafens me, and I put my hands up to my ears. She just keeps shooting, over and over. Then, when the gun begins to make clicking sounds, she uses the empty gun to beat the man's face into a bloody pulp. I've never seen anyone as angry, as out of control, as she is. Tears of frustration well up in her eyes, but none fall.

"Mira," I say gently. "You're not going to kill him that way. He'll still be alive when we phase out of the Quiet."

She goes on with her grisly attack until the gun slips from her fingers. She turns to me, the tears falling now. She brushes them away impatiently, clearly embarrassed that I've seen her lose control like this. "I know that—trust me, I know. It doesn't make a fucking bit of difference, anything I do to them. But I needed that." She takes a breath, pulling herself together. "And now we have to run."

"Wait," I say. "Can you please explain to me what's going on?"

"These fuckers' friends just kidnapped me," she says, pushing her way through the rest of the 'dead' man's three companions.

"What? How?"

"They're after Eugene," she says, running even faster up the stairs. "They're taking me hostage in case they don't find him at home. They want to use me to smoke him out. Only, he *is* home."

"What do they want with him?" I ask, confused. Eugene is one of the nicest people I've ever met. I just assumed this whole kidnaping business with Mira had something to do with her gambling adventures. The four men sure look like the same kind of guys as the one we ran into at the sushi restaurant yesterday. Why would they be after Eugene?

"I don't have time to explain, Darren," she says, and stops on the second floor. She turns to me and sizes me up, as though looking at me for the first time.

"Listen," she says, "I won't make it to the next floor, let alone the apartment. I'm about to fall out of the Mind Dimension—I can already feel myself slipping. Me running here was a desperate attempt. Even if I didn't pull you in, I wouldn't have made it. So, I need your help."

"Of course—what do you need?" I'm scared. I haven't seen Mira like this before. Sarcastic—yes; angry—a couple of times, sure. Even amused. But not vulnerable like this.

"You have to promise to save my brother."

"I will," I say, and it comes out very solemn. "But can you tell me what's going on?"

"Okay, pay attention. I might not have the time to repeat it. I need you to go into the Mind Dimension, the Quiet as you call it, as soon as my time's up. Once you're there, once you've stopped time for everyone around you, you have to come back up these stairs and go all the way to the apartment. Take one of their guns on the way—" she points at the men downstairs, "—and shoot the door lock to get into the apartment. Pull Eugene in to join you in your Mind Dimension. Tell him these guys are on their way up." She says it all in one breath, wiping her eyes and nose with her sleeve. It might be disgusting from anyone else, but somehow Mira makes even this display endearing. "If you pull this off, if you get him out of this fucking mess, I'll be forever in your debt."

"I'll do it, Mira," I say, beginning to think coherently. "I promise, I'll get him out of the building. I'm parked right outside. It shouldn't be a problem."

"Thank you," she says. The next moment, she's next to me. She hugs me, and I clumsily hug her back. I don't know how to act around a woman in such distress. I pat her back gently, hoping it makes her feel better.

Then she stands on her tiptoes and kisses me. The kiss is deep and desperate, her lips soft against mine. It's completely unexpected, but I return the kiss without a second thought, my mind in complete turmoil. So much for coherent thinking.

"Tell Eugene I'm sorry," she says, pulling away after a few moments. "Tell him this is my fault. I led them here. They picked me up at the gym, and I had some mail on me."

"The gym?" I say, a sick feeling in my stomach.

"Yes. I'm so fucking stupid. I took the mail out of the mailbox in the morning. They found it on me. Our address was on it," she says bitterly.

"Your gym is how my friend found you," I admit. "You used one of your older aliases there. I'm so sorry. I should've told you that."

"No, you didn't know the danger we're in. This is definitely on me. I should've asked you how you found me. And I should've changed gyms. We should've fucking moved a long time ago—"

"Where are you now, and more importantly, who are these people? You have to tell me before your time is up," I interrupt urgently.

"The men in this building are working with the ones who picked me up. I don't know for sure, but I think they're all involved with the people who killed our parents. The same Russian crew. The same

Pusher is probably pulling their strings. Eugene can tell you more. I'm in the car where the friends of the assholes downstairs put me. At first they knocked me out somehow, maybe with chloroform or a shot. I don't remember. I don't have any bruises, so I doubt they hit me on the head. When I came to, about twenty or so minutes after, I Split and Read the driver. They gave our address to someone, which led to the group that came here. They work quickly; I didn't expect them to already be here. The ones holding me are going to this address in Sunset Park." She hands me a little piece of paper. I commit the address on the paper to memory. "After that, I Split again and ran here on foot. But it was too far. If I hadn't run into you——"

I phase out before she's able to finish her last sentence. Suddenly I'm standing downstairs again, next to the still-closing door.

Mira is gone.

As she instructed me, I instantly phase into the Quiet.

I run, even though rationally I know I have plenty of time. Unlike Mira, I can spend an insanely long time in the Quiet.

As I'm running, I digest the fact that after she pulled me in and her time ran out, I got pushed out. This is something I wondered about—what happens if you pull someone in, but then get out of the Quiet yourself. Looks like your guest in the Quiet is tied to you. If you get out, they get out.

My contemplation of the rules of this bizarre new world is interrupted by the people on the stairs. The guy in the leather jacket is back, standing there like nothing happened—which makes sense, since nothing actually has happened, at least not outside Mira's Quiet session. I take his gun as she suggested. I'm very tempted to Read them, but I decide to do the important part first.

I run up to the fifth floor. As I turn into their hallway, I see Eugene. He's wearing a ratty hoodie with dorky pajama pants underneath. I fleetingly wonder what happened to the white coat.

He's throwing out the garbage. I don't need to shoot the lock off their door after all.

I touch him, and in a moment he's staring at me, confused.

"Eugene, Mira is in trouble," I tell him instead of hello.

"What? What do you mean?" He looks alarmed.

"Please let me explain. She was just here, in the Quiet. She said she was kidnapped. She said they're after you."

"Who's after me?" He looks panicked now.

"What are you talking about?"

"Come with me," I say, figuring a picture is worth a thousand words. "I'll tell you what she told me on the way down. You need to see them."

"See whom?" he asks, but follows me anyway. "Can you just explain?"

"There are some kind of mobsters who came here for you. I'm taking you to them," I say and pick up speed. "Mira said they're the same people who killed your parents. That some Pusher controls them. She said you would be able to explain this to me."

"And now they have her?" he asks from behind me, his voice low.

"Yes. She's in a car, being taken to a place in Sunset Park. I have the address," I say as we make our way to the four men on the stairs. "This is the problem," I say, pointing at them.

Eugene approaches the men. There is an unrecognizable, almost frightening expression on his face.

Without asking any more questions, he approaches the man wearing a blue tracksuit and touches the guy's temple. I decide to also indulge in Reading, since I'm waiting for Eugene anyway. I walk up to the guy in the leather jacket whose gun I didn't need.

* * *

We're driving to the address we were texted. We're happy we called shotgun, as Boris, Alex, and Dmitri are still bitching about having to share the backseat. Alex, who sits in the middle, apparently spreads his knees too wide for the others' comfort.

Haste was of the essence when we got the call, so we had to leave the restaurant, bill unpaid and food unfinished, and get into Sergey's car. Top priority and all that.

"Wait here," we tell Sergey—the driver—in Russian. I, Darren, understand this again, though the words sound foreign in my mind.

Next, we hand Sergey our phone with a picture of the target. If the target happens to waltz into the building behind us, Sergey is supposed to text us immediately.

I, Darren, am able to feel a more pronounced mental distance between myself and my host, whose name is Big Boris. I'm less lost in the experience, and I'm glad about that. I guess I'm getting better at this Reading business. His mind seems less of a mystery to me with this little bit of extra distance.

Encouraged, I try to focus on how he—or I, or

we—got the idea to come to this building. Specifically, I'm looking for more details on this phone call he/I/we were recalling. All of a sudden, I'm there.

We're at the restaurant eating lamb shish kebab when we get a phone call. We look at the phone and see the number we memorized long ago, and the name 'Arkady' on the screen. A piece of meat gets stuck in our throat. It's the boss, and he always makes us nervous.

"Go to the location I'm going to text you immediately," he says, and we promptly agree.

We're not done with the meal, but we don't voice our annoyance to the boss. Not into the phone, and not even to the crew as we tell them what's what. We wouldn't dream of crossing Arkady; he's the craziest, toughest, most ruthless son of a bitch we've ever met.

I, Darren, repeat Arkady's phone number to myself over and over, so I can remember it in case it comes in handy later. Luckily, I'm very good when it comes to remembering numbers. Still, I need to write this down, along with the address where Mira is being kept, as soon as I can.

I realize that I managed to jump around Big Boris's mind without the usual feeling of lightness. Though with hindsight, I think I did feel light; it was simply on a subconscious level, like I was on a strange mental autopilot. I'll need to play around with this some more, this jumping about in people's minds, but now is not the time. I need to jump out of this mind and get Eugene out of this mess.

*　*　*

When I'm out of Big Boris's head, Eugene is staring at me.

"I couldn't find any confirmation that these men are the same people who killed Mom and Dad," he says.

"That's not the thing to focus on right now," I respond. "We have to get you out of this first. Then we have to rescue Mira."

"Sorry, you're right." He shakes his head like he's disgusted with himself. "There's no time to think about revenge—not that I'm in a position to do anything to them right now anyway. I'm not good at thinking under pressure."

"It's fine. But we have to be careful," I tell him, remembering what I just saw. "Their driver knows what you look like."

"I got that much out of Boris," he says, pointing at the short stocky guy in the tracksuit whose mind Eugene just Read. I internally chuckle, realizing the reason Big Boris needs the 'Big' distinction. He's the second Boris in the group.

"Walk with me," I say. "I want to show you where I'm parked."

As I lead Eugene to my car, I ask, "Is there a back exit from your building somewhere?"

"Not that I know of," he says, scratching his head as we stop in front of my parked car.

"How about a way to the roof?"

"That's through the sixth floor," he says, pushing his glasses further up his nose. "I think I can get there if I need to."

"Okay. Hopefully you won't have to. First, we need to try for the main door. They're walking up the stairs. It will take them time to get to your floor. I have an idea follow me," I tell Eugene and head back to the building.

I run up the stairs, pushing the mobsters out of my way. Eugene follows. I pull the elevator door on the second floor. It's locked. I run to the third floor and do the same thing, getting the same result. The door on the fourth floor opens. So far, so good. I keep running, checking near the elevator doors on every floor until we get to the top, on the sixth.

"Okay, Eugene. Here's my plan: they think your elevator is broken. That gives you a good chance. As soon as I phase out and you're in the real world, press the elevator button. Since the elevator's on the fourth floor, it should get to you in plenty of time. No one is by the elevator on any of the other floors, so there's little risk of any slowdowns."

"Got it, Darren." He smiles for the first time since I've seen him today. "You know, I could've come up with this plan on my own. You're basically telling me to take the elevator down and walk out."

"Yeah, I guess I am. Also, pull up your hoodie and try to hunch as you walk out. Go straight to the car. That's where I'll be waiting, keeping it running," I say. This sounds doable, but I wouldn't want to be in Eugene's shoes right now. "If something goes wrong, run for the roof and text me. I'll phase into the Quiet and come talk to you. Can you phase in every few seconds and walk down to check on the bad guys' progress?"

"Yes," he says. "Since I'll only be spending a small fraction of my available time in each instance, I should be able to re-enter the Mind Dimension without waiting a long time in-between. Thank you."

"Thank me when this is over," I say and begin to walk down the stairs again. He continues to follow me.

"Darren," he says when we reach my frozen body in the lobby. "If something happens to me, promise you'll help Mira."

"I promise," I say. I have no idea how I'll do that, but it occurs to me that the last thing Mira made me promise was that I would save him if she didn't make it. Maybe it wouldn't be so bad having a sibling after all, the way these two look out for each other.

"Don't look guilty as you get out of the building," he says, looking in the direction where Sergey, the driver, is waiting for his comrades.

"Same to you," I say. "See you in a few minutes."

We shake hands.

I take a breath and touch my frozen self on the forehead. The sounds of the world come back.

CHAPTER SIXTEEN

I do my best to avoid looking suspicious, in case Sergey is watching me from the car. I pat my pockets, take out the car keys, and confidently walk back. The image I'm trying to project is: silly me, I forgot something in the car. I might not win an Oscar for my acting, but hopefully the performance will be enough to keep us off the Russians' radar.

As soon as I'm in the car, the first thing I do is fish out the pen I used to sign the receipt for this car rental and the receipt itself. On the back, I write the address and phone number I kept in my head.

Then I start the car.

I've never been this antsy. I stare at the car's

digital clock, but it seems to have stopped. It feels like half an hour has passed when a single digit on the clock advances one minute.

The plan initially seemed simple enough—just wait for Eugene. I didn't expect the suspense to be this torturous. I take a deep breath and mentally count to thirty. It doesn't work.

There *is* something I can do, though, so I phase into the Quiet.

I'm in the backseat of the car. My frozen self is in the front. I've always wondered how the body I get in the Quiet decides where to show up. Of course, there is Eugene's mention of this possibly not being a real body. That still doesn't answer it completely. Whatever I inhabit now, who decided it should appear in the backseat? How did it get there? Why not show up, say, outside the car?

I open the door and get out. Now that he can't see me staring, I can get a better look at Sergey. He seems to be bored, so I assume I didn't raise his suspicions. Good. I also note the car he's driving is actually pretty nice—a Mercedes, no less. Apparently crime does pay.

I walk into the building. The goons are now approaching the second floor. It's scary how close they're getting to Eugene.

I run all the way up to the fifth floor.

Thankfully, I see Eugene opening the elevator door. This is it. The plan is working.

I go back to the car and phase out.

The noises are back, and the digital clock in the car is supposed to work normally; only it's still crawling. I wonder if using the Quiet messes with your time perception. I mean, how long can a few minutes last?

After what seems like another half hour of worry, but really is only three minutes according to the clock, I phase into the Quiet again. Eugene is still not out of the stupid elevator on the second floor.

I go back, phase out, wait ten seconds, and go back in. I repeat this a couple of times until I see the elevator door open. Yes! Finally.

Since I'm here anyway, I walk up to check on the mobsters. They're between the fourth and fifth floors. Satisfied, I go back to the car to phase out again.

Another few seconds, and I can't take it anymore. I phase into the Quiet yet again. Eugene is walking to the door in the lobby. His hoodie is pulled up all the way. His hunching is terribly fake, but as long as he doesn't look like himself, we should be out of this mess in a few seconds. I go back to the car and get out of the Quiet again, only to return a few seconds later.

Eugene is walking toward me. Sergey, the driver, is looking at him with too much concentration. Oh, no. I walk up to the car and touch Sergey's temple.

* * *

We're looking at a strange guy who just left the building in a very suspicious manner. He's trying to hide his face, so we can't see it, but we think he could be the target. Since we know we're here on Arkady's orders, we have to cover our ass. We take out our phone and text Big Boris about seeing something suspicious. Now it can't be said that we fucked up.

* * *

Done Reading the driver, I run back to the car and phase out. I swivel the steering wheel. My foot is on the gas. I shift the gear in the drive position. Then I phase into the Quiet again.

Eugene is a few steps away from the car. I walk up to him and touch his wrist. A moment later, another Eugene stands next to me, this one fully animated.

"I made it," he says on a big exhale, like he's been holding his breath this whole time.

"No. We're far from out of this. Sergey, the driver,

just recognized you."

"Fuck. What do we do?"

"You'll jump into the car, and as soon as you close the door, I'll step on the gas. Buckle up as soon as you can—it might be a bumpy ride."

"Thank you again, Darren," he starts saying, and I wave dismissively.

"As I said before, thank me once we're out of this." Hurrying back to the car, I take a deep breath and phase out of the Quiet.

The next few actions happen in a blur. Eugene runs to the door and jumps into the car. As he closes the door, I stomp on the gas pedal, and we're at the first intersection in seconds.

As we pass the next intersection, I realize that I have no idea where I'm going, but it doesn't matter as long as it's away from that building. On a whim, I decide to keep going straight, and pump the gas again.

I'm going fifty miles per hour when I see the next light turning red a few feet away.

I'm forced to phase into the Quiet. This time, it's particularly eerie. I've never done this in a moving car before. The sounds of the engine, which was working overtime to get us moving faster, are gone. That's strange enough, but what's weirder is that the car itself is standing still. Everything in my brain tells me it should at least move a few extra feet according to the law of inertia, but it doesn't. It's as still as a rock.

I realize I should've done this phasing business at the last intersection. Or even the one before that. It's too late now, though, so I might as well get on with it.

This gives me a chance to check for any pursuers. I walk out of the car and look inside. Through the front window, I see expressions of sheer horror on both my own and Eugene's faces. I walk to Eugene's side and reach into the window. Touching his neck makes Eugene's Quiet incarnation show up in the back seat.

"Darren, what the fuck are you doing? You can't Split like this, in the middle of a car chase."

"Why not?"

"Well, for starters, when you get back, you increase the chance that you'll lose control of the car."

"We'll have to chance it—I'll be careful," I promise. "I had to do it because there was a red light at that intersection."

"Shit," Eugene says, following my gaze. Though here in the Quiet the light is actually dead, he doesn't doubt my powers of observation. And I'm sure he finally understands: the red light means we'll need to stop, and stopping is not a good idea when you've got a car full of very bad Russian dudes on your tail.

"Let's split up," I say. "I'll check out this intersection, and you go back and check on our new Russian friends."

"Okay," he says, turning around and running back toward his building.

I walk more leisurely to the intersection. Eugene has more distance to cover, and I want to give him a head start.

When I'm standing under the traffic light, I turn left and observe the road.

The closest car is about half a block away. I walk toward it. It's a small car, but that doesn't fill me with confidence. Small or not, if it T-bones us, it will hurt.

I open the car door. The speedometer is unreadable— another example of defunct electronics in the Quiet.

I Read the driver. Through his eyes, I learn that he's going thirty miles per hour. I also learn that he's late and is about to speed up. It's unclear what the final speed will be, but I believe he's about to give a noticeable push on the gas.

I make some quick estimates and decide that this

guy will prevent me from turning right or going forward. I'll have to at least slow down at the intersection and make sure his car passes.

On the plus side, the car behind this one is a block away. Since I still have a little time while Eugene does his recon, I run to that car and learn its speed as well. It's also going thirty, but its driver isn't in a rush. He's the type of safe driver who slows down a little before getting to an intersection—which is rare, but admirable.

I walk back to my rental and spot Eugene running back. I have to say, I'm impressed with his speed.

"It's not good, Darren," he says when I'm within hearing distance. "They're in the lobby already, and Sergey's ready to pursue us."

"Damn it," I say, resisting the temptation to kick the car in frustration. "I have bad news, too. We have to actually stop on that light. At least to let this one reckless asshole through."

"Okay, but after that, if the path is clear, we need to go," he says urgently. "I Read them some more. They indeed have orders to kill me—and for running and causing them a headache, Big Boris has decided to make it slow if he gets the chance."

"Then it sounds like we don't really have a choice," I say, trying not to wonder what Big Boris would do with *me*. I'm not on the hit list, but I bet to him it would be guilt by association with equally dire consequences. "There's another car after the one that's the problem, but I think I can make it. Just tell me, should I turn right here or go straight? Do you have any idea where we're going?"

As I ask the last question, I realize that I should've brought it up much sooner.

"There's one place we can go," Eugene says. "Mira and I aren't welcome there. It's the community where Readers in Brooklyn live. It's a long shot, but I can't think of anyone else who could help. They're located on Sheepshead."

"And Sheepshead is where, exactly?" I'm forced to ask. My Brooklyn geography isn't very strong. All I know is the Brooklyn Bridge and, as of recently, Mira and Eugene's apartment.

"Go straight for a bit, then turn left on Avenue Y. It will be a wider street that we'll approach after a few more blocks. Once on it, we go straight, then right on Ocean Avenue. Straight from there until you hit the canal, after that you have to turn left . . ."

"All I got is that I'm going straight for now. Give me a heads up a block before we get where I need to turn."

"Okay," he says. "We should Split again shortly and see where they are at that point."

"Good plan," I say and approach the car.

"Careful," he reminds me.

I take a few breaths and prepare for getting back into driving. I even get into the car in the back, hoping it reduces the disorientation I might get somehow. I touch the back of my head, and the next moment I'm in the driver's seat of the car, my foot instinctively moving from the gas to the brake.

The braking is sudden, and my sushi lunch threatens to come back up. As soon as the car with the guy in a rush passes, I slam the gas again and go on red. The car behind the one that we let through is approaching, but we clear the intersection safely.

We get lucky on the next couple of streets—the lights are green. It's a miracle that we haven't killed a pedestrian. In Manhattan, we would've definitely killed someone by now. People there jaywalk left and right.

"Avenue Y is next," Eugene reminds me, though I actually saw this one coming courtesy of alphabetically ordered street names. We just flew by W, and this one is X.

"It's yellow," I say, looking ahead. "It'll be red by the time we get there."

"Let's repeat what we did last time," he suggests, and I immediately agree.

I phase into the Quiet and pull Eugene in with me. We split up the same way we did the last time.

As I reach Avenue Y, I see that we're about to have a big problem.

There are too many cars here to safely repeat our earlier maneuver.

I Read the minds of the drivers who'll be closest to the intersection by the time we arrive. It seems like no one is in a rush, or plans to speed. But it doesn't matter—we still won't make it.

"They're already approaching Avenue T," Eugene says when he gets back.

That means they're five blocks away.

"How fast are they going?"

"They're insane—pushing a hundred miles an hour. You saw the Mercedes they're driving."

Our luck is just getting worse. My piece-of-shit rental would be pushing its limits if I tried going that fast, even if I was willing to risk it—which I'm not.

"Can we afford to wait for the light to change?" I ask.

"Not according to my calculations. We have to run the red light, and we have to turn right on the next street. We need to get off this main street so they can't easily catch up with us. It's my mistake. I should've had you turn and zigzag the streets earlier."

"I guess we'll need to phase out regularly and time

the turn just right," I say doubtfully. It sounds like we don't have a choice.

The next minute is probably the most nerve-wracking of my life.

I phase in every second, check the intersection, and come back to the car. Over and over. It's hard to drive when you come back, and it's impossible to calculate this whole thing exactly. Still, I think—and Eugene verifies—that I can make the turn if I slow down just a tiny bit to let the Honda closest to us pass by.

The phasing out makes this process play out slowly, like a frame-by-frame sequence in a one-second-long movie stunt.

The Honda gently kisses our back bumper. Brakes screech all around us. I phase into the Quiet to learn what the other drivers will do in reaction to the chaos about to take place. Meanwhile, I also learn what they think of my maneuver, me, and all my ancestors. Out of the Quiet, they express their frustration with a deafening orchestra of honking. That cacophony of car horns and swearing is followed by a loud bang.

The Beemer we just cut off ended up getting rear-ended by an old station wagon. I feel a mixture of guilt and glee. Though no one is visibly hurt, the accident is my fault. On the flip side, however, this might actually slow down our pursuers.

I push the gas and turn the wheel to the right, getting off Avenue Y as Eugene recommended.

"I can't believe we made it," he says. "Now we need to go a roundabout way, and Split to check on our tail."

On Avenue Z, I turn again, and we reach Ocean Avenue uneventfully. The only issue is that we're unable to find our pursuers in the Quiet. At least, not by looking a few blocks behind. We take it as a good sign. We must have lost them.

"Now drive to Emmons Avenue and turn left," Eugene says. "You can't miss it."

He's right. I'm soon faced with the choice of either driving into some kind of canal or turning.

"It's not that far now," he says as we drive a few blocks down Emmons, following the water. I'm glad we're not being pursued at this point; this area is full of traffic.

"Make a left at that light," Eugene tells me. "We're almost there."

Before I get a chance to actually turn, however, the passenger-side mirror explodes.

CHAPTER SEVENTEEN

I phase in, and the noise of the busy street stops. I pull Eugene in with me. As we exit the car, we start looking around.

"Darren, look at this," Eugene says. He sounds more scared than I've heard him since we started this whole mess.

He stands a few feet to the right of the car and points at something in the air. When I take a closer look, my heartbeat spikes. It's a bullet. A bullet frozen in its path. A bullet that just missed the car. The sibling of the one that must have shattered that mirror.

"Someone's shooting at us," I say stupidly.

Eugene mumbles something incomprehensible in response.

Coming out of our shock, we frantically search the cars behind us. It doesn't take long to find the source of the bullets. Not surprisingly, it's our new friends.

How did they manage to get this close? How could I be so stupid—why hadn't I checked on them for so long? Why was I so convinced we'd lost them?

"Eugene, we need to get to wherever it is we're going. And we need to do it fast," I say.

"It's very close. If we turn now, we'll almost be there. Just a few more blocks."

"It might as well be miles if they shoot us."

I've never been shot at before, and I hate the feeling. I'm not ready to get shot. I haven't seen enough, done enough. I have my whole life ahead of me—plus all that extra time in the Quiet.

"Darren, snap out of it." I hear Eugene's voice. "Let's see if we can make this left turn."

Assessing the situation, we quickly realize that our chances of making this turn unscathed are very small. A Jaguar is coming toward us on the opposite side, driving at thirty-five miles per hour—and we'll likely crash into it if we take a sharp left turn. Still, we don't overthink it. A car crash with a seatbelt and an airbag beats getting shot. I think.

I walk to the car, take a calming breath, and phase out. As I'm pulling the wheel all the way to the left, I try my best not to phase into the Quiet out of fear.

With a loud screeching noise, my side of the car touches the Jaguar's bumper. The impact knocks the wind out of me, but the seatbelt holds me, and the airbag doesn't activate. Happy to have made it this far, I slam the gas pedal harder. The car makes all sorts of unhappy sounds, but at least we made it through that deadly looking turn relatively unscathed.

When we're midway through the block, I phase in and get Eugene to join me.

We look at our handiwork back at the beginning of the street. As a result of our crazy turn, the Jaguar hit the Camry in front of it. Its bumper is gone, and the once-beautiful car is pretty much totaled. I think the guy inside will have to be hospitalized which I feel terrible about. Furthermore, the entire intersection is jammed with cars. Unless they plan to go through them, our trigger-happy friends can't pass.

Still, Eugene walks over to Read Sergey's mind, just in case.

"Darren, I'm such a fucking idiot," he says, slapping his hand to his forehead.

"What is it?"

"They know where we're going. Their boss texted them the address. That's how they caught up with us. I should've realized that if they're working with a Pusher, he or she would know the location of the Readers' community. That they would know we're likely to head that way."

"It's too late to blame yourself now," I tell him. "Let's just get there."

"I'm not sure we'll make it. Sergey plans to ram this car." He points at the tiny Smart Car that happens to be the smallest of those involved in the jam, and I realize that we have a problem. Our pursuers can go through the blocked intersection after all.

"We already have a little bit of a head start," I say, trying to summon optimism I don't feel. "We'll just have to make it."

"Okay," Eugene says. "From here, we can actually walk to our destination on foot before we get back into the real world. This way, you'll know the exact way there."

We take the walk. I realize we'll make it when we see the wall of the gated community that is our destination. Whether Sergey rams that car successfully or not, we can do this.

We're a mere three blocks from where we need to

198

be.

When we get back to the car, I phase back out.

I push the little rental to its limits. I'm going eighty, the tires screeching as I make the next turn. I hear the loud bang behind us and know that Sergey followed through with his plan; the Smart Car is probably toast by now.

It's too late for our pursuers, though. We've reached the gate that separates us from our destination. I stop the car in the middle of the street and am about to phase into the Quiet when I'm pulled in instead by someone else.

"Eugene, you beat me to it," I say when everything goes still. Only when I look to my right, I don't see Eugene.

I see someone else—someone I've never met before.

CHAPTER EIGHTEEN

The guy is holding a huge military knife. Threateningly. I don't know what to make of it, since we're in the Quiet. I'm not sure what will happen to me if he uses the knife on me. Not that I care to find out. He doesn't look like someone who makes idle threats. I make a mental note to find out the risk of death in the Quiet. I know injuries don't stick. And yes, I cut myself to find out. Wouldn't anyone? My shrink thought it was 'interesting' that I cut myself in my delusional world—I recall her talking some nonsense about the physical pain helping me deal with some fictitious emotional one.

"I've seen that one before," the guy says, pointing

the knife at frozen Eugene. "But who the fuck are you?"

I gape at him. I don't know what to make of his muscular build, short haircut, and military clothing. Is he some kind of Reader security guard?

"I'm only going to ask one more time," he says, and I realize I didn't respond to his question.

"My name is Darren," I say quickly. "I guess I'm a Reader."

"You guess?"

"Well, it's new information to me, so I'm not used to announcing it. Eugene and Mira are the first Readers I've ever met."

The guy's eyebrows lift, and he unexpectedly chuckles. "I've got news for you. If what you say is true, then today—right now—is the first time you've met a real Reader. Few of the people inside consider the Tsiolkovsky orphans that."

"You sound like you consider them Readers, though," I say on a hunch.

"No one gives a rat's ass what I think; I'm just a soldier. But I say if you can spend more than a second in the Mind Dimension and can Read a single thought, you're a Reader. I'm a simple person with simple definitions, I guess. Who cares how you got to be that way?"

"That makes sense," I say. "I'm sorry, I didn't catch your name."

"You didn't catch it because I didn't give it," the guy says, all traces of amusement gone. "It's Caleb. And knowing my name isn't going to help you, unless you have an explanation for what you and Eugene are doing here. This is private property."

"His sister Mira was just kidnapped. Eugene barely escaped getting killed. There are men coming after us as we speak," I try to explain. "Or at least they'll be here once we leave the Mind Dimension."

"How many?" he asks, coming to attention. The bit about Mira seems to have made an impression.

"There are five of them. They're driving a Mercedes; they could be here any second."

"What else should I know about them?" Caleb asks, his hand tightening on the knife.

"They're some kind of a Russian gang or something. Sergey, two Borises—"

"I don't give a shit what their names are," Caleb interrupts me. "If they're armed and heading this way, we won't be bonding on that level."

"Okay," I say. I have a bad feeling in the pit of my stomach.

"Stay here and don't move. Sam and I have sniper rifles pointed at your heads. If you so much as sneeze, we'll blow your brains out."

I don't have a clue who Sam is, but it doesn't look like Caleb's interested in answering questions right now. As I'm trying to come to grips with his threat, he leaves the car, and in a minute I'm forcefully phased out of the Quiet.

"Eugene, don't move," I say hurriedly. There's a red laser dot on his chest, as though someone has a gun pointed at him—which is apparently the case.

"Why?" he asks, confused.

I phase back into the Quiet instead of answering. I'm afraid of even talking while someone is pointing a sniper rifle at me. What if Caleb thinks my lips moving qualifies as movement and shoots? When I find myself in the backseat again with the world silent, I pull Eugene in.

"I just spoke to some scary-looking dude who's guarding this place. He pulled me in," I explain.

"Did whoever it was say they'll help?"

"Not exactly. He said not to move and that they have guns pointed at us." I swallow. "I saw a laser pointer on you."

"I see," Eugene says, surprisingly calmly. "We'll probably be okay. They'll most likely go Read our pursuers to verify you told them the truth."

"And on the off chance they don't?" I ask, though

I can guess the answer.

"In that case, they'll let us resolve our differences with the people following us."

"Great. And we're supposed to just sit and wait?"

"I know I will. The Readers don't usually issue empty threats. If you were told not to move, don't move."

Annoyed with Eugene's ironclad logic, I phase out.

I sit without moving for about five seconds, until I realize that waiting next to Eugene's building earlier was child's play compared to this. I count twenty Mississippis before I phase in. The Mercedes is halfway between the corner where Sergey rammed that car and our current location. The fancy car is barely dented, but Reading Sergey's mind, it seems he doesn't agree with my assessment. He's furious about the damage to his car and determined to make us regret this chase, if he gets the chance. Reading the mind of his friend Big Boris, I get the feeling they'll have to get in line when it comes to doing evil things to us.

I walk back and phase out. I'm now back in the car, waiting for whatever it is that's about to happen.

After what seems like a couple of hours, I think I hear a car motor. As soon as I do, I also hear a gunshot.

I automatically phase in this time. My brain must've thought that shot was directed at me, and this is a near-death experience.

I get out of the car and look at my frozen self. No gunshot wounds. That's good. The only abnormalities about my frozen self are the humongous size of my pupils and the overly white shade of my face. The whole thing makes my frozen self look ghoulish. Eugene is even paler and is holding his head defensively. Like his hands can somehow protect him from a bullet.

I look around. The front end of the Mercedes is visible at the head of the street. I walk closer and realize its tires are in the process of blowing out. They must have been shot.

In a daze, I walk back and phase out.

The sound from the tires exploding reaches my ears now, followed by the screech of steel on pavement as the car continues to careen forward on the exposed rims. Another burst of shots are fired, and I phase into the Quiet again.

This time, just like the last, I didn't intend to phase in. It just happened under stress.

I get out of the car. My frozen self doesn't seem to have any blue in his eyes anymore, his irises swallowed up by the black of his pupils.

I walk to the Mercedes. When I look inside, I wish

I hadn't.

I've never seen anything like this before. I mean, I've seen dead bodies in the Quiet, but not of people who were actually dead—or about to be dead—outside the Quiet. This is very different. Very real. These five people have bloody wounds in their chests, and their brains are blown out all over the car.

I feel my gag reflex kick in like I'm about to throw up, but nothing comes out. I'm not sure if it's even possible to puke in the Quiet; it's never happened to me before.

I feel bad about these men getting killed, which is a paradox, given that they were just shooting at me a few minutes ago. I think it has something to do with having Read their minds, like it bound us in some way. There's nothing I can do about it, though; they're gone now.

"Rest in peace," I mutter, walking back to my car. I morbidly wonder what I would experience if I Read one of them right now. Or more specifically, I wonder what I would feel if I catch someone at the right—or wrong—moment, and end up experiencing death firsthand?

I shake my head. I'm not doing that. Besides, I might experience that for myself when I get out of the Quiet; Eugene and I might be the next two targets Caleb shoots.

On the plus side, the Mercedes has no more tires at all. The added resistance should counteract inertia to prevent them from ramming into us—in theory. I'm no expert on blown-out tires.

I walk back to the car and phase out.

A few more shots fire in a blur, and the Mercedes moves a few more feet before it screeches to a stop on its rims. It didn't reach us by at least a hundred feet, but I still feel the need to swallow my heart back into my chest.

Things get suspiciously quiet for a few nerve-wracking seconds, and then the gate shutting us out of the community starts to open.

The guy I met before, Caleb, steps out, with a couple of other dudes who look pretty badass. One of them is toting a sniper rifle. I'm guessing that means he's Sam. He and this Caleb guy look like twins, with their stony, square-jawed faces and hard eyes. Sam is a bit taller, which makes him just short of enormous.

"Darren, Eugene, come with me," Caleb says curtly, and I see Sam shoot Eugene an unfriendly look.

"What about that?" Eugene says, gesturing at the car riddled with bullet holes. He's pointedly avoiding looking at Sam, which I find interesting.

"Both it and your ride will be taken care of. No one will ever find them, or those bodies, again," Caleb assures us.

I manage to feel grateful for having the foresight to say yes to the optional rental car insurance, which seems a bit shallow under the circumstances, even for me.

"Wait," I say, remembering the rental receipt. "I need to get the address where Mira's being kept. It's in the glove compartment."

Caleb walks to the rental and gets the paper I need.

"Here," he says, handing it over to me. "Now, no more delays. We need to have a chat."

And with that, under gunpoint, we enter the private Reader community of Sheepshead Bay.

CHAPTER NINETEEN

We're taken to some kind of ritzy clubhouse. It's in the middle of an impressive-looking housing community. A house here must cost millions. I didn't even know a place like this existed in Brooklyn—it's more like something you'd expect to see in Miami. Such a lavish compound sort of makes sense, though; Readers should be able to find a bunch of creative ways to make money given their abilities. Or, more accurately, our abilities. I need to get used to the idea that I'm a Reader, I remind myself, remembering the snafu with Caleb earlier.

Inside the clubhouse are an indoor pool, a large fancy restaurant, and a bar. Caleb takes us further in, into what looks like some kind of meeting room.

A dozen people of different ages are here, looking at us intently.

"That really is Eugene," says a hot blond woman who looks to be a few years older than Mira. "I can vouch for that."

"I knew that much," Caleb says, but finally lowers his weapon. "And this guy?"

"Never seen him before," she says, looking at me. I do my best to keep my eyes trained on her face, rather than her prominent cleavage. Being polite can be a chore sometimes.

"He learned about being a Reader yesterday," Eugene explains. Then he gives the blond woman a warm smile. "Hi Julia."

The woman smiles back at him, but her expression changes back to one of concern quickly. "Are you sure he's a Reader?" she says, sizing me up.

"Positive," Eugene says. "You know my family history with Pushers. It was the first thing I checked."

"You have to forgive me, but I must verify for myself," Julia says. "You can be too trusting, Eugene."

So these two somehow know each other. This must be what Eugene was talking about when he said things are less strict in modern New York than they were in Russia during his father's time. Despite being 'exiled,' Eugene and Mira are not completely cut off from other Readers.

"Bring in our bartender," Julia says to a short young guy to her left. He leaves and comes back with a young, extremely pretty woman a few moments later.

"Stacy, I just wanted to tell you about my new guest," Julia says, gesturing toward Eugene. "Put his drinks on my tab."

"Sure thing, Jules," the woman says. She probably expected something more meaningful, being summoned as she was. Stacy begins to walk away when I'm suddenly in the Quiet again, and the woman who knows Eugene—Julia—is standing next to me.

"Now, Darren, I want you to Read Stacy," she says. "Tell me something about her that no one else can know, and I'll know you're not a Pusher."

This reaffirms what I surmised earlier: Pushers can't Read at all. Otherwise, this test—and the test Eugene did when we first met—wouldn't make sense.

Without much ado, I walk up to Stacy and touch her temple.

* * *

We're walking into the room with Julia. *Oh shit, he's here*, we realize, looking at Caleb. Of all the times we've made a fool out of ourselves, the time we got drunk with Caleb is hardest to forget for some reason. Probably because he's a real man, unlike the rest of the guys here. It's mostly a bunch of rich mama's boys in this community. Well, except for Sam and the other guards.

I, Darren, try distancing myself from Stacy, the way I did in the now-dead Sergey's mind earlier. I latch on to her memory of something involving Caleb, and try to remember what happened. I also notice that the feeling of lightness coming over me is overwhelming this time. If I feel any lighter, I might actually start floating.

"Caleb, you can't drink that as shots. It's sacrilege," we say, watching our favorite customer down a shot of uber-expensive Louis the XIII Cognac like it's cheap vodka.

"How am I supposed to drink it?" he says, giving us a cocky smile. "Show me."

"Are you buying?" we say. "I can't afford a three-hundred-dollar shot."

"Sure," he says. "How much for the whole bottle?"

We grin at him. "You don't want to know. My suggestion would be to switch to good vodka."

"What's good?"

"Try this," we say, pouring a couple of shot glasses of Belvedere, the better of the two pricey vodkas they stock in this place.

We take a shot glass ourselves and cross arms with Caleb, planning to have our shot poured into his mouth, and hoping he does the reverse. "How about a toast?"

When we see the expression on his face, our heart sinks.

"I'm sorry, Stacy. I wasn't trying to hit on you," he says, gently pulling away.

Goddamn it. Not this again. What's wrong with the men in this fucking community? We know most others are probably just rich snobs, but Caleb is their security. What is his deal? And Sam's? It's like a girl can never get laid around here.

I, Darren, distance myself again. I feel a little gross. After all, I'm in the head of a girl who's clearly lusting after this guy. What's worse, from Reading her, I completely understood what it's like to want to take a guy home. I need to get out of Stacy's head, fast.

* * *

"Okay," I tell Julia when I'm out. "I think I have something to convince you. She wanted to sleep with him." I point at Caleb. I stress the word 'she' too much, and Julia smiles at my discomfort.

"You men and your homophobia," she says, walking over to Caleb.

In a moment, Caleb's double appears, the animated version of him looking at Julia curiously.

"He says that Stacy was interested in you," Julia tells him.

"That's his proof?" Caleb says, grinning from ear to ear. "That sounds more like an educated guess to me."

"Right, because every woman wants you?" Julia says sarcastically.

"You tell me."

"Not if you were the last man on the planet," Julia retorts sharply.

"Louis the XIII Cognac," I say, tired of their back-and-forth. "Three hundred dollars for a shot; vodka shots; turning the girl down. Any of that ring a bell?"

Caleb's face turns serious. "I do remember that now," he says, frowning at me. "But it doesn't make sense. It was months ago."

He stares at me intently, like he's seeing me for the first time. Julia is also staring. Then they exchange meaningful looks.

"Okay, Darren," Julia says, looking back at me. "You have to be one of us."

She walks toward herself and touches the frozen Julia's cheek.

The world comes to life again.

Julia looks from me to Eugene, then back to me, waiting for Stacy to leave the room. When the bartender is finally outside, the short guy who went to get her closes the door.

"Darren's one of us," Julia says. "I can vouch for that. He's not Pusher scum."

Everyone seems to relax. There had been tension up to this point, but that tension is gone now. They *really* dislike Pushers over here. Given what Pushers did to Eugene's family, and what I suspect they did to my own parents, I can't really blame them.

"That still doesn't explain what that half-blood degenerate is doing here," Sam—Caleb's annoying doppelganger—says. A few people nod their heads and murmur their agreement.

"Watch it, Sam. Eugene is my personal friend," Julia says, staring the guy down. Sam sneers, but keeps quiet. When Julia turns away, however, the look he gives Eugene is even more hostile than before.

"My sister has been taken," Eugene explains, ignoring Sam. "And I think Pushers are behind it."

This last statement gets everyone's attention, even the asshole Sam's.

"Why would Pushers be after Mira?" Caleb says, his eyes narrowing. It sounds like he knows her.

"They're not after her—they're after me," Eugene explains.

"Is this a continuation of that story you told me about your parents?" Julia asks.

Sam scoffs. "You mean that crazy conspiracy theory—"

"Shut it, Sam," Caleb cuts him off. "Let's get the facts without needless commentary."

I can tell Sam is dying to talk back, but decides not to. I guess that means Caleb outranks him or something.

"Please start from the beginning," Julia says to Eugene. "Tell everyone what you told me."

Looks like I was right earlier. There's definitely some kind of history between her and Eugene.

"I believe," Eugene says, giving Sam a hard look, "that my parents were killed because Pushers were trying to kill my father and me."

"Why would they want to do that?" Caleb asks.

"Because of my father's research. He was working on some things they would've found unnatural," Eugene says, and there's anger in his voice. "He was trying to figure out how Reading and Splitting into the Mind Dimension work in the brain."

The room grows tense again.

"That kind of research is forbidden," Sam says harshly, frowning.

"It's not forbidden," Julia corrects him. Like Caleb, she seems to have some authority around here. "As long as the research is never published and is only discussed with peers who are Readers themselves."

"My father was very discreet. Very few people knew what he was working on," Eugene confirms. "I believe something about his research made Pushers think that Readers would gain a big advantage if he succeeded."

"And would we?" an older woman asks. She's been quiet up until now, but from the way everyone looks at her, I can tell she's important.

"I'm not really sure," Eugene says. "I don't know the practical applications of what he was doing—but I imagine so. Any good science has real-world benefits."

"Eugene is more interested in theory, Mom," Julia tells the older woman. "He's above politics."

"So they're trying to kill you because you inherited the same research your dad was doing?" I decide to butt in.

Everyone looks at me with surprise. They probably assume I already know what's going on since I came with Eugene.

"Exactly," Eugene says. "When I used that first test on you to see if you were a Reader, I did it using the method Dad developed back in Russia. The fact that they tried to kill me today is extra evidence he was killed over his work. They missed killing me that day. I was shopping for groceries." He stops and takes a deep breath. "For those of you who don't know, my parents were murdered when their car exploded right in front of our house. My sister was coming back from school—she saw the whole thing."

Julia walks over to him and puts her hand on his shoulder. Her mother frowns, and Sam looks furious. I wonder if he has the hots for Julia, or just hates Eugene because he's a 'half-blood.'

"Was there any proof of his words in the minds of those men you killed outside?" Julia's mother asks.

"Kind of," says Caleb. "Sam and I checked them thoroughly. There were signs of Pusher activity in the mind of the driver. He drove their boss someplace, and the Pusher made him forget what he heard when the boss spoke to the Pusher on the phone. We couldn't get a visual on the Pusher, of course."

"The fact that there's a Pusher involved is good enough reason to help them as far as I'm concerned," Julia says.

"Right. The fact that his sister slutted around the Russian mob has nothing to do with her capture," Sam says, sneering again. I really don't like this guy. If he wasn't so big and scary-looking, I'd strongly consider punching him in the face.

"Mira was trying to find the people who killed our mother and father," Eugene says defensively. "I told her not to, but she wouldn't listen to me."

"Mira isn't someone who'd be easy to control," Caleb says, chuckling. Is that admiration I see on his face?

"Well, if you ask me, the simpler explanation for the kidnapping would be his sister's gambling debt," Sam says. "As to the original explosion, it's more likely that his father's 'friends' from Mother Russia had something to do with it. Isn't that more plausible than some crazy theory about Pushers?"

"I think the Pusher used the Russian mob for that very reason—so that the police would think the explosion had something to do with what my dad did in Russia," Eugene says, his face turning red with anger. "Only that's bullshit; Dad was the most honest and peaceful man I've ever met."

"Okay," Julia says. "We can debate this until the cows come home, and it won't solve anything. The only way to figure out what's really going on is to rescue Mira—which is what I think we should do."

"Julia, you need to consult your father on this," Julia's mom says, and Julia frowns at her.

"She's right," Sam says. "Jacob would never want to get involved in these exiles' business."

"Well, let's find out, why don't we?" Julia suggests, and walks over to a desk to get a laptop.

CHAPTER TWENTY

"What are you going to do?" Julia's mother asks.

"Skype with Dad, if that's what it takes," Julia responds, turning on the laptop.

As her video call is connecting, Julia motions for Eugene and me to come closer. We gather around the computer, and I see a middle-aged man with tired, beady eyes appear on the screen.

An expression of distaste crosses his stern face as he sees Eugene.

"Hello, Jacob, sir," Eugene says respectfully.

"Hi Dad," Julia says.

"Hello," I say politely.

"Who are you?" Jacob asks, staring at me.

"This is Darren, Dad," Julia says, "a new Reader we discovered."

"A new Reader?" he says, watching me intently. "You look familiar to me, kid. Who are your parents?"

"He doesn't know who they are," Eugene jumps in, and Jacob's face reddens at the sound of his voice. I'm glad Eugene volunteered this information because, as embarrassing as it is, I don't know the last names of my parents. Just their first names: Mark and Margret. I need to find out their last names when we're out of this mess. For all I know, I could have extended family in this very room.

"Everyone knows who their parents are," Jacob retorts, but he's not looking at Eugene. He's still boring into me with his beady eyes. "But we'll continue this conversation another time. For now, I'd like to know what this call is about," he says, turning his attention to Julia, "as well as what he—" he gestures at Eugene, "—is doing in our compound."

"Eugene needs our help, Dad," Julia explains. She then proceeds to tell her father a much smoother, more plausible version of the theory about Eugene's parents. She's good. She downplays the research Eugene and his dad worked on, which appears to be controversial in this community. She highlights the

Pusher involvement every chance she gets. "So I want to help them and learn more about this matter," she says in conclusion.

"Hell, no," her father says, catching me completely by surprise. "I thought I forbade you from ever consorting with that half-blood."

"This has nothing to do with my personal life; it's about standing up to the Pushers," Julia says, glaring at her father. Her face takes on a rebellious look, making me remember my own interactions with Uncle Kyle.

"My decision is final," Jacob says. "I want him out of the community. He should be grateful our security saved his life. If I had been at the compound, that would not—"

Before Jacob gets a chance to finish his last sentence, Julia closes the laptop with an angry bang.

This seems like as good a time as any for me to phase into the Quiet, and I do.

When everything is still again, I look around. Julia is clearly pissed. Her mother's expression is neutral. Though Sam is standing a bit to the side, he clearly heard the conversation because he looks grimly satisfied.

It's interesting to contemplate the fact that in this room, everyone could be doing what I'm doing right now, at any time. Are people watching me frozen as they do so? It's hard to imagine myself standing there, not moving, not thinking, as someone else goes about his or her business while I'm none the wiser.

Shelving these thoughts for later, I touch Eugene's forearm.

"What do we do now?" I ask him when he joins me in the Quiet. "That was a huge flop."

"I don't know what to say," Eugene says. "I didn't really have a clear plan."

"This Julia, how do you know her? She seems to be sympathetic."

"We had a class together in college. Then, for some reason, she agreed to date me." He smiles ruefully. "But when her father found out my status, he freaked out. He's very traditional."

"And this is supposed to be more open-minded than Russia?"

"That I'm alive is testament to that," Eugene says. "I thought we might have a chance at getting help here because Jacob hates Pushers more than anyone. Under normal circumstances, anyone even remotely in trouble with Pushers automatically becomes an 'enemy of his enemy' kind of friend."

"Except you," I say, looking at him.

"Right. I think my history with Julia hurt our

chances. The problem is, this is Mira's life on the line, not mine."

"If you don't mind, I want to talk to Julia some more," I say, unwilling to give up.

"Go ahead," he says. He looks over at her, his face drawn. There's something in his eyes, in the way he watches her, that tells me he's far from over her. Then he shakes his head, looking away. "I'm not sure if it's going to help, though."

Instead of arguing, I walk over to her and pull her in.

"Darren." She smiles at me. "I was about to Split to talk to the two of you. It looks like you beat me to it."

"It's funny how that works," Eugene says. "I have this time-slicing algorithm I developed that simulates—"

"Eugene, I'm so sorry about my dad," Julia interrupts him gently. My guess is that she wanted to stop a science diatribe. I suspect it's not the first time she's done this. "Let's talk about what we can do for Mira, if you don't mind."

"After the conversation with your dad, I thought you wouldn't be able to do anything to help," Eugene responds, science forgotten as worry shadows his face again.

"I'm going with you," she says. "Together, we'll get her out of whatever trouble she's in."

"No," Eugene protests. "That would be too dangerous—"

"I'm doing this." She gives him a steely look. "I've had enough of people telling me what to do."

"No, Julia, I don't mean to tell you what to do." Eugene immediately backtracks. "I just worry about you, that's all . . ."

Her icy glare warms considerably, and she takes a step toward him.

"With all due respect," I interject, "how can you help us, Julia? This sounds like a job for someone like that." I point at motionless Caleb.

"I'm good at getting into places I shouldn't—picking locks, that kind of thing," Julia says, turning to look at me. "It's a skill that could come in handy in exactly the type of mission I imagine this will become. But you're right, we need Caleb or one of his people. We have to convince him to help without my dad's orders."

"How do we do that?" Eugene asks.

"Can we pay him?" I suggest. With the stock options I got at the gym, money will soon be easy to come by. Even easier than it usually has been for me.

"If you're talking about money, it won't work,"

Julia says. "But there are other forms of payment."

"What are you suggesting?" Eugene looks puzzled.

"Nothing sinister." Julia grins. "You see, your friend Darren seems to have impressed Caleb. Actually, he impressed both of us with his Reading Depth."

"Oh?" Eugene says, and I recall that this is a sensitive subject for these people. Something like asking about the size of someone's paycheck or his package were the analogies used, I think.

"What does my Reading Depth have to do with Caleb?" I ask.

"Caleb is obsessed with improving his fighting skills," Julia says. "He's already rumored to be the best fighter among the Readers. Still, he's always looking to get better."

"I'm not going to fight him, if that's what you're about to offer," I say, shuddering. I'm not a fan of violence, plus I'm not suicidal. The guy will probably kill me before I get a single punch in.

Julia laughs. If she weren't laughing at my expense, I would say her laugh was nice. In general, she's a very pretty girl. I can see why Eugene likes her, and I can tell that he truly does. I'm less clear why the reverse is true, but it must be, as I catch her giving him decidedly warm glances. It's weird—I always thought geeky types like Eugene didn't do well with women. Of course, this is based solely on my friend Bert, which isn't exactly a valid statistical sample.

"No, Darren, thank you for offering, but I'm not asking you to fight Caleb," she says, still having a hard time keeping a straight face. I'm insulted. How does she know I'm not secretly some Kung Fu master?

"You have an amazing Reading Depth," she continues. "You can offer to take him into the mind of some famous fighters. I suspect he would find the idea intriguing."

Eugene looks from me to her uncomfortably. "But—"

"Eugene, please, I'm trying to help save your sister," Julia interrupts, and Eugene falls silent, his expression smoothing out.

"Can someone actually do that? Bring another person into someone else's mind?" I ask, wondering what Eugene had been about to say. He'd seemed worried about something for a moment.

"Yes," she says, "absolutely. It depletes your power even faster than pulling someone in, but from what I saw, you won't have a problem with that."

"Why can't Caleb do this himself?" I ask. "Why can't he Read some fighter's mind on his own?"

"For all his fighting prowess, Caleb isn't very powerful when it comes to matters of the Mind Dimension," Julia explains. "He can't go back very far at all with his Reading, and he can't do it very often, which is exactly why such an opportunity might appeal to him."

I consider questioning her further to figure out what made Eugene uncomfortable, but then I decide against it. "Fine, I'll do it," I say instead. I can't see any other way to help Mira at the moment, and I find the idea of doing this fighter Reading thing rather intriguing. If Caleb is doing it to get better at fighting, does it mean that by joining him, I could get better, too? Or, more accurately, will I actually learn how to fight as a result of this?

"Great, Eugene, let's go so they can have some privacy," Julia says, grabbing his arm and pulling him back toward their frozen bodies.

"I don't know how to thank you for this, Darren," Eugene says on his way to his frozen body, and I shrug in response, still unsure what the big deal is.

As soon as they phase out, I walk up to Caleb and pull him in.

"Darren," he says with a smirk. "To what do I owe the honor of being pulled into your own personal Mind Dimension?"

"Julia said you might be able to help us, for a

price," I begin, and Caleb laughs.

"Did she now? And what did Julia think would be my price?" His grin reminds me of a hungry shark.

"She said you like fighting, in all its forms," I say, hoping I don't sound crazy. "She said I can take you into the mind of a couple of fighters as payment."

"Interesting," he says, crossing his arms. "And did she say anything else?"

"No, just that."

"You really did just learn how to Read yesterday, didn't you, Darren?" he says, still grinning. "What Julia 'forgot' to mention to you is that very few Readers would agree to offer me this kind of deal."

"Why?" I ask, wondering if I'm about to learn the reason for Eugene's concern.

"Because it's considered a private, almost intimate experience to pull someone else into a Reading," Caleb says, his grin fading. "You get glimpses of the other Reader's mind, and vice versa."

"Oh." I try to keep my jaw from dropping. "What does that feel like?"

"I only did it once," he says, completely serious now. "But that time, it was incredible."

I stare at him for a moment, then shrug. "I don't care," I say. "To save Mira, I'll do it. I'll let you get inside the heads of a couple of people of your choice."

Caleb looks like a happy shark again. "We have a deal then," he says, smiling widely. "I'll let you know whose minds I choose."

Why do I feel like I did something reckless just now?

"Oh, don't make the long face," he says, apparently sensing my sudden unease. "I promise not to deplete your Depth. We both know you can go back very far, so getting to see a few fights shouldn't be a problem at all. We won't see how these men began their careers, only something fairly recent."

"Okay, sure." I decide to worry about it later.

"Good. Now pull Eugene and Julia back in."

I do as he says.

"Here's the plan, people," Caleb barks, taking control of the situation. "Eugene and Darren will leave, looking exceedingly disappointed. Julia, I'll meet you in the parking lot after I get the supplies I'm going to need. We'll pick you gentlemen up on Emmons Avenue."

"Who else is coming with us?" Julia asks. "Not Sam, I presume?"

"You presume correctly," Caleb says. "It will be just me."

"Just you?" Julia frowns.

"Oh, ye of little faith." Caleb smirks at her. "One of me is probably overkill for this mission."

"Yeah, yeah," she says. "I don't doubt your machismo, Caleb; I just want the girl to survive the rescue."

"She will," Caleb assures her. "You have my word on that."

"Okay, then let's get back to our real lives," Julia says.

"Hold up. Darren, there's something you should know," Caleb says, turning toward me. "I've known Mira for a while. She's a good kid. I was going to offer to help Eugene anyway—especially since I knew Julia would do something reckless, and Jacob would hold me liable for her actions regardless of my involvement. Not to mention, I like a good skirmish."

"So I didn't need to agree to this deal?" I say dryly, and he shakes his head.

"Nope. You didn't. But a deal is a deal." He winks at me. "I'm really looking forward to all this."

* * *

Leaving the community with apparent dejection, Eugene and I make our way to Emmons Avenue, to the exact place where we caused the last car crash. There are still bits of plastic and glass on the asphalt, but the broken cars have apparently been towed.

I'm deep in thought, trying to understand how I got involved in all this craziness.

"Darren, about taking Caleb into someone's mind," Eugene breaks the silence.

"He already told me; you see into each other's minds," I tell him.

"Oh, good. I'm surprised Caleb was so honest," Eugene says with relief. "Julia should've warned you. She can be kind of ruthless when it comes to getting what she wants."

Before I can reply, we're interrupted by a loud car honk. It's a Hummer—occupied by Caleb and Julia.

Of course Caleb drives a Hummer, I think as I get in.

"Give me that address, Darren. We have a damsel in distress," Caleb says.

I give him the address, and he sets his GPS to the location. With a roar, the Hummer is off, moving through the streets of Brooklyn like a tank.

CHAPTER TWENTY-ONE

We park in a Costco lot in Sunset Park.

According to Google Maps, the place where they're keeping Mira is an industrial warehouse. What these guys are doing so far from Brighton Beach, none of us have a clue. Brighton Beach is where the Russian Mafia is supposed to be headquartered, according to Eugene. I hope that this actually plays to our advantage. If they do call for reinforcements, it's a twenty-minute drive without traffic, according to Julia's phone. Of course, that assumes the reinforcements are on Brighton Beach, and—this is a big one—that they're going to need reinforcements against the four of us.

Caleb jumps out of his seat and starts rummaging through the trunk of the Hummer.

"Are we shopping for supplies?" I ask, looking in the direction of the huge store. I'm only half-joking.

"I have everything I need," Julia says, hanging a messenger bag over her shoulder.

"They don't sell the type of stuff I need in Costco," Caleb responds, putting what has to be a rifle in a special carry case over his shoulder. "At least not in New York."

He puts on a vest with special pockets and straps the huge knife I saw previously to it, along with a couple of handguns.

"This is for you," Caleb says, handing me a gun.

The seriousness of the situation hits me again. We're going against armed criminals. Just the four of us. A scientist, a girl whose toughness I haven't fully determined yet, and, let's face it, a financial analyst. Caleb is the only person even remotely qualified for this rescue. Despite his unshakable confidence, the odds don't seem right to me.

Not to mention, the people holding Mira have an ace up their sleeve: a hostage.

All we have is our unusual skill set.

Caleb clearly has a plan, though. He leads us to an abandoned warehouse located a short distance from where we parked.

We walk up to the top floor, and Caleb methodically unzips his gun case and starts setting up. The gun is huge and looks very professional—complete with scope and silencer. I wonder if this is what he used to gun down our pursuers earlier. Eugene and Julia, who have been silent for some time, exchange impressed looks. Eugene seems grimly determined, while Julia looks thoughtful.

I gaze around the room we've found ourselves in. It's dusty and dark, despite large, floor-to-ceiling windows—probably because said windows are yellow and covered with grime. Caleb opens one of those windows, lies down on the floor, and aims the huge gun at the industrial warehouse across the street. Then he says curtly, "All right, Darren, pull us in."

I leverage my natural anxiety over what's about to happen and quickly phase into the Quiet. Then I touch everyone in turn, pulling them in.

Once we're all in, we walk down the stairs and cross the road. This part of Brooklyn is so abandoned that being in the Quiet doesn't seem like much of a change. At least not until we cross the road, and Caleb breaks the door with a series of kicks. Even in a scarcely populated area like this, such bold breaking and entering might've gotten us noticed and reported, if it took place in the real world.

"You know, I could've picked that lock," Julia says, looking at what's left of the door on the ground.

"You'll get your chance," Caleb tells her as he walks into the building.

We walk through the door and find ourselves in a large open space. There are a bunch of guys frozen in the process of walking around. They all have guns. Caleb walks between the guys and the windows, looking intently at the building we came from.

His plan is beginning to dawn on me.

He's figuring out how to shoot them from our location across the street. He's triangulating his shots; as soon as we phase back out, he'll shoot.

I'll have to remember to never piss off Caleb.

"Where's Mira?" Eugene asks after examining the hangar.

"Try Reading them," Caleb says without turning. "We need to figure that out, because once we get back to the real world, the information will be lost."

Right. Because you can't Read dead men. A chill skitters across my spine. Caleb is too calm about it. Too poised. His coldness makes me uneasy. I wonder if I, personally, am capable of killing. Even if it's an enemy. Even in self-defense. I don't know, and I hope I don't find out today.

For my Reading target, I choose a big guy near one of the columns. He must be on steroids or growth hormones—or both. Though he's my height, he must be at least two hundred pounds heavier than I am. Being that he's Russian, I wonder if he's trying to look like a bear. He's closer to a gorilla. I catch myself hoping that Caleb doesn't miss this specific dude with his rifle. We wouldn't want to face him in anything but a gunfight.

Putting my hand on his gigantic forehead, I jump in a few hours ago.

* * *

We see Mira playing cards with Vasiliy. There is one other guy in the room with her.

"Na huy ti s ney igrayesh?" we say. As usual I, Darren, marvel at understanding this. He, Lenya, was asking a question about why his idiot bro is playing cards with the hostage. Playing cards with a girl who is a renowned card cheat.

He, Lenya, is picturing what he would do with the hostage. We see images of Mira tied up and abused. I, Darren, distance myself almost instantly and nearly puke—though this is not easy to do in my current position. Can you vomit mentally? This almost makes me want to jump out of this asshole's head, it's so sick. I also feel an instinctive need to protect Mira from ever coming near this guy. I feel dirty. The best way to describe the experience is it's as if I'm dreaming of being this scumbag. I am rethinking my earlier squeamishness toward killing.

I shouldn't jump out, however, as he's about to give me key information. I try to focus on what the guy's body is experiencing—an ache from yesterday's workout, soreness in the knuckles from punching someone, anything except those sick rape fantasies. This approach is flawed, though, because focusing on his body makes me realize he's getting turned on from these disgusting thoughts. Thankfully, before I'm forced out of his head from sheer horror, he refocuses on what he should be doing. And that is locking the door in front of him from the outside.

We lock the door, mentally praising Tolik, who is also in the room. At least he has his gun next to him, and isn't letting the bitch distract him. He also forbade untying her legs from the chair. Tolik will keep Vasiliy in check.

We walk out into the corridor and through a maze of concrete hallways until we reach the stairs. Then we go down to the main hall, where the rest of the guards are.

I, Darren, now know where Mira is being held.

I almost jump out, but I decide to try to go even deeper. I want to know who told this guy to lock the door from the outside. That's very specific. Whoever came up with that could've been trying to limit Mira's range of motion in the Quiet—and thus might be the Pusher fuck behind all this.

I jump further.

We're sitting in a banya. I, Darren, learn that a banya is a Russian spa—a bit like a sauna, but much hotter. Given how we, I mean he, feels when in there, it sounds like something I should check out.

I go further still, jumping around scenes from this goon's life.

Aha.

"Keep those doors closed," Piotr says. We look at Piotr and wonder who the fuck he is to be giving orders around here.

I, Darren, realize with disappointment that Piotr is another Russian I saw in the very room we're in now.

I jump out of Lenya's head.

* * *

"Darren, let's go," Caleb says as soon as I'm conscious of being myself again.

"Give me a minute," I respond. "I need to check that guy." I point at Piotr, sitting at a desk.

"Hurry," Caleb says.

I walk up to the guy. He looks a tiny bit more intelligent than the one whose mind I was in a moment ago. I place my hand on his forehead.

* * *

I'm in, but I don't know where to start. Intuitively I jump around scenes from this guy's life until I find it.

We're watching boxing on TV when another mind enters. Time stops; now there are more of us in his head.

I understand that the guy himself wouldn't have felt the Pusher enter his mind. Apparently people don't consciously notice either us or them when we do our thing. But I am very much aware of it. It's like a ghostly presence. And as I keep Reading, the Pusher begins to give instructions.

'Instructions' is a poor word for it, but I can't think of a better one. In reality, they're almost like experiences the Pusher inserts into the guy's mind. Like the reverse of Reading. The Pusher inserts experiences and reactions to them. How this will ensure the guy does what he's supposed to, I don't know, but it must work. To me, it feels a little bit like a very detailed story of what Piotr should experience when the time is right.

The experience in this case is pretty simple. 'Pick up the phone' is the first step. The Pusher seems to almost play out a fake memory for his target. Every detail of how it would be to pick up the phone is considered: which hand, the weight of the phone in his hand, and so on.

Next comes the instruction: 'Text all the trusted people with a request to meet at Tatyana Restaurant in an hour.'

Finally, Piotr is instructed to get up and go there himself.

After that, the Pusher's presence disappears. Based purely on the person's presence in this mind, I can't tell whether it was male or female. To my disappointment, whoever it was never came into physical contact with Piotr.

I Read Piotr's mind a little longer. I'm curious what he'll recall of the Pusher influence. As I expected, he remembers nothing. He arrives at the restaurant, slightly amused. *Isn't it strange how sometimes you drive someplace, but don't even remember the driving process?* he thinks.

It seems like the Pusher's influence has caused a mild memory lapse in the target's mind, but overall Piotr acts as though of his own volition. It's interesting to watch how he rationalizes his actions as happening of his own choosing and his memory lapse as one of those times when the conscious mind goes on autopilot and the subconscious takes over. The illusion of free will at its finest. It comes to me all over again how dangerous these Pushers are. Whatever they need done, all they need to do is plant the seed in someone's mind.

Mind-rape, Eugene called it. Now I understand why.

Knowing I won't get any more than this, I decide to jump out of Piotr's mind. People are waiting for me.

* * *

When I'm conscious again, Caleb is standing next to me looking like he's about to say something snide. I just head for the exit, explaining where Mira is as I move. The group follows.

"That's perfect," Caleb says when I finish my explanation. "If they're that far inside the building, they definitely won't hear my shots."

"Did any one of you Read a guy whose name was Arkady in there?" I ask. No one responds, so I assume they haven't.

We return to the room across the street, on the top floor near the window. Our frozen bodies are hunched near Caleb, who's lying on the floor with his eye to the scope of his rifle. I touch my forehead.

As soon as the phase-out process is complete, Caleb fires the first shot.

Then another.

Then another.

I lose count of the shots, as I'm more focused on plugging my ears. In the movies, silencers work much better than in real life. Despite the elongated device on the end of the barrel of Caleb's rifle, the noise is deafening in this room. I hope the area is abandoned enough that no one hears the shots—or if they do and call the cops, we're out of here before they arrive.

His shooting done, Caleb pushes off the floor to a standing position.

"Now things should go more smoothly in there," he says, picking up his gun. Wiping down his prints, he leaves the rifle behind and heads for the stairs.

We follow him all the way down to the ground level of the building we've just fired the shots from.

"Darren, take us into the Mind Dimension again," Caleb orders before we exit to the street. "We need to assess the situation."

"Okay, Sergeant," Julia says sarcastically. "Before we go running around again, can you please tell us the plan?"

"The plan will become clearer after we reconnoiter," Caleb says curtly. "The only thing I can tell you now is that with two armed guards in the room with Mira, stealth is of utmost importance. If I were them, I'd shoot the hostage as soon as I caught wind that some shit was going down."

Eugene looks pale, and a shudder runs through me. Without further ado, I phase into the Quiet once again and get everyone to join me.

We cross the street. I'm getting a sense of déjà vu. The door is locked again, which of course makes sense, but is no less annoying.

"Now you can practice picking the lock," Caleb says to Julia. "We want to be in as quickly as we can."

She goes inside her messenger bag and takes out what I assume are the instruments of a professional burglar. I wonder where she learned to do this. Her people seem too ritzy for thieving.

She struggles with the door for only a minute before we're in.

"Will you be able to do this faster when we actually get here?" Caleb asks.

"Yes. I can get it down to twenty seconds," she says.

We enter the hangar we inspected before. Though I'm not surprised by what I see, my gag reflex kicks in, and I barely hold back vomit.

They're all dead. Shot in the head, every single one of them. There's blood, lots of blood everywhere. Though it's my second time seeing a scene like this today, it's not in any way less disturbing.

Julia looks green too, making me feel a bit better about my own sorry state.

Caleb steps over the bodies in his way and just waltzes to the stairs. We gingerly follow, trying to keep our eyes off the dead people.

After a few flights of stairs, we reach a floor that appears to be the one we're searching for. We follow Caleb into the maze of corridors, which, according to Lenya's—the disgusting gorilla's—memories, leads to the room where Mira is held.

There's a guy standing with his back to us at a bend in the corridor, looking toward the door. Another is standing by the door, looking at the hallway. This means there's no way for Mira to come out of the room, nor for us to turn the corner without one of these men raising an alarm. Not good.

"Okay," Caleb says. "We'll need to take these two guards out. Darren, Eugene, this one is yours," he says, pointing at the guy with his back toward us.

"Ours?" Eugene appears confused.

"You need to overpower him," Caleb explains with a sharp smile. "Silently, so the two guards with Mira don't hear us coming."

Caleb is enjoying this, I realize. Eugene must've acted arrogantly toward him in the past, or maybe Caleb is just a sadistic prick. Whatever the case, Caleb is clearly trying to shock the guy. Or is it my buttons he's trying to push?

"I can turn the corner and quickly grab the guy. When he can't move, you stab him," I propose, looking at Eugene.

"Good plan," Caleb says, glancing at me with approval. "I have some extra knives for you gentlemen."

Eugene doesn't seem as hesitant as I would expect at the prospect of stabbing someone. Have I misjudged him? After all, just because someone is a little geeky doesn't mean he can't be tough. Or score a hottie like Julia, I remind myself.

"What are *you* going to do?" Julia challenges Caleb.

"I'll take care of that one," Caleb responds, nodding toward the guy facing us.

"Wait—won't he shoot you as soon as you turn this corner?" Eugene asks. I know he's walking into some sort of smart-ass remark from Caleb.

Instead of answering, Caleb walks back into the hall leading to this turn. Then he pointedly turns the corner. In a blur of motion, the knife is in his hand; the next moment, after a lightning-fast throw, it's in the second guy's chest.

Show-off.

"Any more questions?" Caleb asks. No one responds. "In that case, Julia, see how fast and how quietly you can pick that lock."

Julia takes out her tools and does her thing. It takes her about a minute.

"That won't work," Caleb says when she's done. "But we'll get back to that in a moment."

Without waiting for an invitation, we all barge into the room.

The room still looks like I remember it. Or more accurately, how the now-dead Lenya—the gorilla—remembered it.

It was originally meant to be some kind of storage room. There are no windows, and the walls are painted a dull white color. In some places, the paint is chipping away.

Just like in the memory I obtained, there's a guy with a gun near him, though now he seems to be playing with his phone. It's a little odd, since his phone has a pink case. Just like before, there is Mira, tied to the chair, playing cards with another guard. Only unlike before, they're all frozen in the midst of their activities.

I walk up to Mira and touch her forehead.

As soon as she phases in, her eyes look like they're about to jump out of their sockets. She has an expression on her face I don't recognize. Then I get it—I've never seen her this genuinely happy to see me before. Her eyes scan the room, and she sees Eugene. Her face lights up.

"You did it," she says, turning toward me, and I hear the joy and disbelief in her voice. "You saved him. I don't know how I can thank you."

"I said I would," I say, trying not to think of all the ways I'd want Mira to express her gratitude. For the first time in my life, I understand the motivations of those hero types. For a fleeting moment, I feel like I really did something important. Something impressive. It's a great feeling.

"But what are you doing here?" she says, her expression changing as she fully registers the situation.

"What does it look like?" Caleb says. "We're rescuing you."

"In that case, why did you bring Eugene?" She looks at me like I'm an idiot, and all my heroic feelings deflate. Like I could've stopped a brother from trying to save his little sister?

"It's too dangerous," she says, turning toward Eugene. "You shouldn't have come." She looks from Caleb to Julia to me. Then at the corridor through the open door. "This is all of you?" she asks, her shoulders slumping.

"It's going to be enough," Caleb says.

She shakes her head. "This is going to be impossible." She doesn't wait for anyone to respond before she walks out of the room. She must not realize that we—well, Caleb—already took out the lion's share of her captors.

"As friendly as ever," Caleb says, giving me a wink. "Julia, go out and then lock and unlock this door again. Try to do it quicker and quieter this time."

We stay in the room to judge Julia's work. After the initial click of the lock, the rest of the stuff she does is pretty subtle, but still audible if you know what to listen for. She seems to finish faster this time.

Caleb waves at us to follow him and walks out of the room—to follow Mira, I presume.

"Do it ten more times," he says to Julia on the way out.

The three of us try to find Mira. We walk a couple of floors up. Everything seems abandoned. We find Mira on the seventh floor, punching the wall in frustration.

"What is it?" Eugene asks her.

"That fuck isn't here," she says, punching the wall again.

"Who?" Eugene says.

"The Pusher. The one behind all this. That chicken shit's not here. That was my main hope, the only silver lining to this. I thought he'd be overseeing the whole thing."

"I Read a mind earlier," I say. "The Pusher who influenced that mind was very careful to avoid revealing himself to his target."

"Then this is pointless. You guys should go back and wait. Maybe he'll show up eventually," she says.

"That's not happening," Caleb says, standing between her and the wall she's been punching. "Here is what *is* happening. You'll try to be as loud as possible as soon as you hear any funny sounds coming from outside your door. Talk loudly, ask questions—or even better, fall from your chair. That would distract them *and* get you out of harm's way."

"Yeah, yeah, don't try to teach a fish how to swim," she mutters. Then she takes a deep breath and glances at Eugene before turning her attention back to Caleb. "Look, even with those dead bodies I just saw downstairs, busting in here is going to be dangerous," she says in a more even tone. "Promise me that Eugene won't take part in this. They took me to smoke him out in the first place, so if you bring him, you'll be playing right into their hands."

"Yes, so he told us. We have a deal," Caleb says before Eugene starts protesting. "I won't force Eugene to come with us."

Mira gives him a disbelieving look, but seems a bit calmer as we make our way back to the room. I get the feeling that there's definite history between Mira and Caleb. I don't like it, not one bit. Though it can't be romantic, can it? He's a little too old for her, and he called her 'kid.' Maybe it's a bond between two kindred, sarcastic, pain-in-the-ass spirits?

When we rejoin her, Julia is still diligently practicing unlocking that lock.

Upon Caleb's request, she does a final run, which is extremely quick. She's way faster and much quieter than she was before. For the first time, I'm beginning to think we can pull this off.

"So what's the exact plan?" I ask.

"While Julia works on the door, Mira falls on the

floor with her chair. Then I shoot these two," Caleb says, pointing his index finger in a gun motion at the two frozen guards.

"I'm not sure I can fall like that," Mira says, looking at her frozen self. Her hands are free, but her legs are duct-taped to her chair.

"We'll just have to practice that part as well," Caleb says, his eyes crinkling in the corners. I get the feeling he's going to enjoy this part, too.

"You want to tie me to a chair so I practice falling?" Mira says. She doesn't look happy.

"Exactly." Caleb grins. "See, Eugene, you're not the smartest one in the family."

Eugene and I free the frozen Mira from the chair and place her limp body gently in the corner of the room. I accidentally touch her exposed skin, but nothing happens. I guess once we pulled one Mira into the Quiet, touching her frozen self doesn't produce more Miras. It would have been kind of cool if it did.

Mira sits down in the chair and, muttering something in Russian under her breath, grudgingly allows us to tape up her legs with the duct tape her guards left lying around. She's now set up exactly as her frozen self was a few minutes ago.

She leans her body to the right, but the chair doesn't fall. She shakes it back and forth, and slowly, almost grudgingly, the chair falls over.

"Are you okay, sis?" Eugene asks her.

"Yes. Pick me up," she says, trying to push herself off the floor. Her position looks extremely uncomfortable.

"That was too slow," Caleb says. "Try again."

I get up and walk over to a dingy couch standing in the furthest corner of the room. I take the cushions from it, and lay them on either side of Mira. No point for this to hurt more than it already must.

"Thanks, Darren," she says before she begins shaking the chair again.

The cushions help, but it's clearly an unpleasant practice. She does it again and again over the course of about twenty minutes. We try to give tips—which are usually met with disdain.

Eventually Caleb decides she won't be able to improve further.

About five seconds to fall over is the best she can do.

"We need a different strategy to distract them," I say. "Besides falling, I think you should also start yelling. Scream 'mouse' or 'spider' at the critical moment and start waving your arms, acting like you're freaking out right before you fall."

Julia chuckles. Mira gives me a deadly glare. Caleb

is about to say something, but Eugene shakes his head at him behind Mira's back. He must actually think it's a good idea.

"Just do it, sis," Eugene tells Mira. "It won't be the first time. Remember when you jumped on the table—"

"Don't say another fucking word," Mira interrupts him. "I'll do it."

And before her brother has a chance to say anything more, she quickly walks up to her own frozen body which is now lying on the floor—and touches that version of herself on the cheek. That makes her phase out, and she's no longer in our company.

Only the Mira on the floor remains.

"But I was about to ask her to practice the new strategy," Caleb says with visible disappointment.

I can't help myself. I burst out laughing.

"This is a pretty serious situation, guys," Eugene says, but I can tell he's trying his best to suppress a smile. Despite the danger we're in—or maybe because of it—everyone finds the idea of Mira freaking out like that hilarious. Then again, Eugene implied that she's acted like this before. Maybe when she was little? It's hard to picture it now. I wish I could Read Eugene's or Mira's mind.

We exit the room. Caleb holds the door for everyone, making me wonder why he's being such a gentlemen all of a sudden. As soon as we're all out of the room, I find out.

He's decided to do a little practice on his own.

All I hear is a quiet rustling of clothing, and the next moment Caleb is holding two guns, one in each hand. Two shots fire at the same time. Two men in the room each have a bullet in their head.

I begin to feel even more confident about the success of this mission.

We walk back to our bodies and phase out.

"Any last words?" Caleb says to us all.

"I'm coming with you," Eugene says, his voice filled with determination.

"Of course," Caleb says. "I said I wouldn't force you. But if you volunteer, well, that's a different matter." He hands Eugene a knife. "You're in charge of stabbing the guy in the corridor, remember?"

I get a knife as well. *Great.* As though the gun I was given earlier wasn't bad enough.

We cross the street, for real now. The area is pretty dead, yet it seems infinitely more alive now than when we crossed this road in the Quiet— mainly because all the ambient noises of Brooklyn are back. With the increase in noise, my adrenaline levels go up as well.

Julia picks the lock on the front door in twenty seconds—just as she said she would. So far, so good. We walk through the hangar. My heart rate becomes a tiny bit calmer. This part isn't all that different from the version in the Quiet. The heavy walls block most of the sounds of the city. The dead men are just as frozen in death here as they were in the Quiet.

"Situation check," Caleb whispers when we're near the stairs.

I phase in, and pull everyone else in with me. We walk up the stairs until we get to the corridor and turn the corner again. In the few minutes it took us to walk across the street and through the hangar, the men have not moved; they stand in pretty much the same positions.

"Good," Caleb says. "We'll do another check, right before turning the corner. This will be my signal." He gives us a thumbs-up sign. Not the most imaginative signal, but it gets the point across.

We walk back and phase out. Now we finally get to make the trip up the stairs in the real world.

We all try to make our walk stealthy, but only Caleb succeeds. We get to the corner, and he does his thumbs-up sign. I phase in and pull them all in again. The men are still standing as they were.

"Are you ready?" Caleb says, looking from me to

Eugene.

"Ready," I say.

"Let's get this over with," Eugene says.

I notice Caleb never asked to rehearse this part. I bet I know why: he realizes that if given enough information, Eugene might lose his nerve. Or maybe he thinks I'll lose mine.

We phase out. Everyone looks at me expectantly. I take a deep breath and turn the corner.

My heart is racing a hundred miles per hour, but I ignore it and grab the now-very-familiar Russian as soon as I turn the corner, placing my hand over his mouth to muffle his scream. I hold him as tightly as I can, but he struggles and I know there's very little time.

Out of the corner of my eye, I see Caleb make his move. I can't afford to pay attention to him, though.

I rotate my body, and Eugene is there with the knife. It's unclear if he jabs the guy with it, or if I push the guy onto the knife myself. However, it's quickly clear that it's done—the knife is there, in the man's stomach.

He makes a horrible grunting sound. My own stomach heaves, but I hang tight.

The grunt is echoed by the sounds of another wounded guard—the one Caleb must've thrown the knife at.

The guy I'm holding stops struggling, and I feel him going limp. I don't want to think about what that implies as I let him slide to the floor. Eugene looks pale as he steps back, dropping his knife on the ground.

Caleb is next to the guy by the door already and is holding the man's throat in a tight grip, blocking off air and preventing further sounds.

Julia begins to pick the lock on the door. I walk toward her and Caleb, trying to avoid looking at all the blood.

I hear faint screams inside the room. Mira must have started her performance.

Caleb eases the now-limp body to the floor.

I focus on the good things. The plan is going smoothly.

I try not to think of the gruesome parts.

Not surprisingly, there's a difference between stabbing people in the Quiet and seeing it done in real life. Blood flows. People actually die. The difference is huge. I can also actually throw up in the real world, an urge I fight with all my strength.

Julia is done with the door and looks at Eugene in triumph.

In a split second, her face changes—dread

contorting her features. Her fright is contagious. Instantly I turn, so I can see what she sees.

Eugene is still standing next to the man he stabbed, but what he's not seeing, because he's looking away, is that the guy isn't dead, like we thought. He's lying on the floor and holding a gun aimed at us.

Before I can even digest the image in front of me, there is a shot.

It's the loudest thing I've ever heard. It's like my ears explode. Like the most intense thunder you could ever imagine.

Everything seems to slow, and then goes quiet. A very familiar kind of quiet. I realize that I phased in without consciously trying. Near-death experiences are becoming a habit today.

In the safety of the frozen world, I look around. There is a bloody circle on Julia's left shoulder. Her face is frozen in shock. Despite myself, I'm relieved. Though she's clearly been shot, even without being a doctor I know that shoulder wounds are rarely fatal. The real reason for my relief, however, is that my own frozen body is unscathed.

The biggest surprise is Caleb, who I thought was still in the process of laying the dead guard on the ground. In the time it took me to phase into the Quiet, he's already holding a gun. And the gun has smoke around its muzzle. He must've managed to take it out and shoot, almost as soon as the other shot was fired. Or maybe he saw it coming? Maybe he was phasing in every second, assessing the situation around us—something I now realize I should've been doing. Still, Caleb's speed is astounding.

The most incredible part is that I can actually see the bullet. It's a few inches away from the shooter's head.

With dread, I open the door into the room with Mira.

It's bad.

The guy who was playing cards with her is now standing. He's trying to get out of the way of his partner the more suspicious guard, who's now pointing his gun down at Mira. She, with her chair, is lying on her side on the floor. She completed the difficult maneuver, as we'd planned. Only now it might be for nothing. The noise of the gunshots ruined everything.

I get closer to the suspicious guard and inspect the situation. The muscles in his wrist are taut. He looks like he's about to pull the trigger.

I refuse to accept this.

I touch his forehead.

* * *

We're still contemplating what to say in the text to the hostage's brother, whose number we located in the girl's pink phone, when we hear the shots outside the room.

Someone must be trying to free the hostage. Unbelievable. What idiot would even try something so stupid?

We know we need to follow orders, which were very explicit on this. Arkady made us repeat them. If any shit goes down, first order of business is to shoot the girl. After that, we must deal with whoever might've come after her. If we kill her brother, we get a big bonus.

We take the gun and aim. We're pressing the trigger.

* * *

I get out of his head. I have no doubt about it now. He's shooting. In his head, I felt my—or I should say *his*—finger squeeze the trigger. His brain already sent the instructions to his arm. In a second after I phase out, a shot will fire. A shot aimed directly at

Mira.

If only he was just reaching for his gun. If only his partner would trip and fall to cover her somehow. If only the door was wide open already—I'm right behind it, ready to shoot.

I want to scream. I'm ready to kill. Only it's too late.

I can't just watch Mira die. I have to do something.

Not sure why, I approach the guard who was looming over Mira. The one who was playing cards with her before. Vasiliy, I remind myself.

I touch his forehead.

* * *

We're looking at the girl on the floor. We know what Tolik is about to do. We feel faint regret. We think it's a shame she'll be killed. We think it's a waste of a very nice female specimen.

I, Darren, realize that this one likes Mira in his own crude way. A way that's not altogether different from the way I like her. It makes this experience odd. It also seems to push me further with what I'm trying to do.

Without fully realizing what I'm doing, I focus on

his regret. On the fact that he likes her. Even on his lust for her.

I picture it growing. I picture what regretting losing someone very close to me would be like and channel it into Vasiliy. I recall wanting to fuck Mira and channel those memories into him. I recall what losing my grandmother felt like, which has nothing to do with Mira, but seems useful, so I channel that into him, too. It feels like I'm pouring my essence into him. As if for a moment, we merge into the same person.

It feels like I'm achieving something, so I continue further, almost becoming my host.

I think of Tolik. He's my best friend. If I just get in the way of the gun, he'll never shoot. He'll stop, and then I can talk to him, explain why the girl must be spared. I picture us coming up with a scheme. We tell Arkady she's dead. Tolik gets full credit and a huge bonus. She and I disappear from NYC, maybe even from the US. I picture how grateful the girl will be when she realizes she owes her life to me.

I finally picture the simple action that can make it all come together. I need to fall on top of her. From where I'm standing, it will take less than a second to just fall down.

I will feel her body under my own. I'll be her strong protector. A real man. All I need to do now is show a little courage. And then, of course, Tolik will stop. He'll never shoot me. All he needs to see is that that she's important, and it will all be over . . .

* * *

As if in a trance, I feel almost pushed outside his head. I'm not sure what just happened.

I realize that in reality, there is only one thing I can do. I can open that door, and I can shoot Tolik. And hope I make it—hope I shoot him in time.

My brain screams at the impossibility of making the shot in time, so I try to hope that whatever I did inside Vasiliy's head will help.

I open the door. I push my frozen self out of the way and take his exact position. I close the door behind me.

Now, I try it in the Quiet. A test.

I open the door. My hand is steady. I shoot. His temple is red. It all takes no more than two seconds.

I'm ready. I take a breath and phase out.

I open the door for real this time. My hand is even steadier here than it was in the Quiet.

I hear the Russian's shot as I squeeze the trigger.

CHAPTER TWENTY-TWO

My own gun fires—but I don't hear it. I phase into the Quiet once more.

Tolik's head is frozen mid-explosion. Bits of his skull and brain are caught mid-flight toward the wall behind him. I killed him, but I don't even register that fact. Instead I focus on something else entirely—and what I see makes me feel like I'm about to burst with joy.

Vasiliy, the guy whose head I was in just a moment ago, is on top of Mira.

He took the bullet that was meant for her.

I roll him off her and see no signs of the bullet having traveled all the way through. It hit him in the right shoulder blade.

Mira is unharmed, other than some minor bruises due to falling with the chair. She hasn't been killed.

I know there is a possibility, however remote, that the bullet is still about to go through Vasiliy. I might've phased in at just the right fraction of a second to make the bullet freeze on its way out.

I run to my body and slam into myself, roughly grabbing whatever exposed skin comes my way.

I am in the real world again, hearing the sharp crack of the shot I just fired.

I rush into the room.

I ignore the sound of Tolik's body falling to the floor where I shot him. My entire focus is on Vasiliy, now crumpled on top of Mira.

He moans in pain.

She's quiet.

My heart sinks.

Tolik's shot must've reached her through Vasiliy's body.

Filled with panic, I roll him off her as fast as I can. His moans become screams at my rough treatment, but I barely notice his pain as I see Mira lying there, alive and unharmed.

Just as she was in the Quiet.

She's strangely silent, however, and I decide that

she must be in shock. Feeling a tiny fraction calmer, I start cutting away the duct tape from her legs.

"You're a hero, Darren," Caleb says from the door. For the first time, I hear no sarcasm in his voice. "You should know I don't throw around compliments lightly."

"Help me untie her," I say, not knowing how to respond to that.

"Can't," he says curtly. "I need to bind Julia's shoulder."

I remember Julia's wound and I nod, continuing to work on the tape by myself. Mira still doesn't say a word. Her silence begins to worry me.

Finally, I succeed in cutting through the tape, and Mira slowly gets to her feet, still without speaking. Then, not looking at me, she walks to the gun that fell from Tolik's hand and picks it up.

She's going to finish Vasiliy off, I realize.

But instead of pointing the gun at the injured mobster, she points it at me.

I barely have a chance to register the tears gleaming in her eyes and the shaking of her hand before I instinctively phase into the Quiet.

Battling my shock and disbelief, I approach her and brush my fingers against her frozen cheek, determined to understand her strange behavior.

Instantly a moving Mira joins me in the Quiet. She wipes the tears from her eyes, looking around the room, and as her gaze lands on me, the expression on her face turns to fury. Stepping toward me, she slaps my face, the way wives do to cheating husbands in movies. Then she punches me in the stomach.

I'm stunned. What the hell is she doing?

"You fucking Pusher!" she says through clenched teeth. "Don't you ever come near me again!"

Before I can react, she turns around and touches her frozen self.

Numb, I look at my own self standing in front of her gun. His face looks more confused than it did on the day I first discovered being able to 'stop time.'

I now know what upset her so much.

I now understand what I did to Vasiliy.

Mira must've phased in after the shots went down. She must've Read Vasiliy. She must've seen the telltale signs of what happened in his mind.

Signs similar to what I saw earlier in Piotr's mind.

Signs of what I refused to really think about, until now.

I *made* Vasiliy protect her with his body.

I made him fall.

I overrode his free will.

I *pushed* him.

I'm what she hates most in the world.

A Pusher.

I touch my confused self on the forehead.

I am back in the real world, with Mira's gun in my face. It's shaking more than it did before.

Is this really how it's going to end? Is she going to kill me? I'm so numb that I just stand there, waiting for it.

But no. She slowly lowers the gun. Then, hurrying over to Tolik's dead body, she picks up her pink phone from the table next to him and runs out of the room.

Finally shaking off my strange numbness, I run after her.

"What the fuck was that?" Caleb yells after me, but I don't have time to explain.

I keep running after her, gaining speed, but she's fast. After chasing her down a couple of flights of stairs, I slow down and then stop. Even if I catch her, I have no idea what I'll say.

Feeling exhausted all of a sudden, I go back and rejoin Eugene and Caleb, who seem very confused. Julia is bleeding, her face deathly pale, and Eugene is hovering next to her. His face is almost as pale as hers.

"What's going on?" Caleb asks, frowning at me.

"Don't ask," I say. "Please."

"Is Mira okay?" he persists.

"I think she is, yes," I answer wearily. "I mean, she's not hurt—physically, at least."

"Fine. Then help me," Caleb says. He gives Eugene the keys and tells us to get the car. Meanwhile, he picks Julia up like she weighs nothing, and starts down the stairs. Everything seems to happen in a haze.

Eugene and I get the car in silence. He looks back toward Caleb and Julia once, then looks around, probably hoping to spot Mira. She's nowhere to be seen, but we find the car in the Costco parking lot, where we left it. I drive to the curb, pull up, and Caleb carefully puts Julia in the back. Caleb reclaims the driver's seat, while I ride shotgun. Eugene gets in the back with Julia. I hear them talking quietly, but make out only her repeated insistence that she's fine.

In five minutes, we're parked at the Lutheran Medical Center. Caleb gets out as soon as the car's stopped. He leans in Julia's window. "You holding up okay?"

"Fine," she says. "Really. I'm okay." She doesn't look okay—she looks like she's about to pass out. Eugene doesn't look much better.

"I'll be right back," Caleb says. "Give me a minute."

As soon as he's gone, I hear the sound of Eugene's text alert go off. I don't know why, but the sound alone fills me with dread.

"Darren," Eugene says after a few seconds. "Mira just texted me. She's on her way here on foot. She says she wants you gone when she arrives."

I don't know what to say. "Okay. I'll go then."

"What happened?" Eugene asks, his face the very definition of confused.

"Talk to Mira," I say tiredly. "Please don't make me explain."

We share an uncomfortable silence. Through the haze surrounding me, I'm aware of Caleb returning a few minutes later with a wheelchair for Julia. How did he get one so quickly? Did he show his gun to someone in the hospital? Surely not, or security would be right behind him, I reason dazedly.

Caleb says something to Eugene and sends him on his way with Julia. Something about making sure she's okay and about being back once he drops 'the kid' at his house. He also suggests some bullshit cover story to explain the gunshot wound. I listen, but I'm mentally somewhere else.

When Eugene and Julia enter the hospital, Caleb

starts the car.

"Are you okay, Darren?" Caleb asks me as he pulls out of the hospital parking lot.

"Yeah, sure," I say on autopilot. I'm far from okay, but he doesn't need to know that.

"All right then, I'll take you home. What's your address?"

I give it to him, and he puts it into his GPS.

"Okay, good. Now give me your number, too, and I'll get in touch with you soon. I've almost made up my mind about the first person whose fighting we'll experience."

"Great."

"You're in shock," Caleb says. "It happens sometimes after a battle. Even with the best of us."

I just nod. I don't care about his theories or approval. I don't care about anything. I don't want to think.

My phone rings. It's my mom Sara.

"Do you mind?" I ask Caleb. I think it's very rude to talk on a cell in front of someone.

"No worries," he replies, and I answer the call.

"Hello?" I say.

"Darren, I was beginning to worry," Sara says. This makes my stupor fade a little. Beginning to worry is Sara's default state. I don't believe the woman has ever called me when she was chill. Of course, if she thought I was in even a fraction of the trouble I've been in today, she would go to her second-favorite state—panic about me.

"I'm okay, Mom. I was just busy today." Understatement of the century.

"You aren't mad at us?" she asks, and I immediately realize I've been an ass. I should've called to reassure them about the adoption business from the day before.

"No. We're good, Mom," I say, forcing certainty into my voice. Better late than never, I always say.

She seems to believe me, and we move on to the usual 'how are you' chat that we have every day. The whole thing is surreal.

When I get off the phone, Caleb is just a few blocks from my place. We ride in a companionable silence the rest of the way.

"This is you," Caleb says when we get to my building.

"Thanks for the ride," I say, extending my hand to Caleb. "And for helping us out. That was some good shooting you did."

He shakes my hand firmly. "You're welcome. You weren't bad yourself, and I know these things. Get some sleep," he says, and I nod in agreement.

It's the best idea I've heard in a long time.

I get to my apartment, eat something, shower, and get into bed. Once there, I just sit for a moment, looking outside. It's still light out there, the sun only beginning to set. I don't care, though. I'm exhausted, so I lie down.

When I'm this tired, time seems to slow. It's like my head approaches the pillow in slow motion.

I think about everything that's happened to me today. I think about the things that are about to happen. In those couple of seconds it takes for my head to hit the pillow, I think of anything but the fact that Mira will hate me now. Anything but the biggest question of all.

What am I?

And then my head finally touches the pillow, and I'm out, falling asleep faster than I have in my entire life.

SNEAK PEEKS AND FREE BOOKS

Thank you for reading! If you would consider leaving a review, it would be greatly appreciated.

Darren's story continues in *The Thought Pushers (Mind Dimensions: Book 2)*, which is available at most major retailers.

Please sign up for my newsletter at www.dimazales.com to learn when the next book comes out.

Also, Anna and I currently have two FREE ebooks out: *The Sorcery Code*, an epic fantasy novel, and *Close Liaisons*, an erotic sci-fi romance. Please check out the samples and links for these freebies below.

I love to hear from readers, so be sure to:
-Friend me on Facebook:
https://www.facebook.com/DimaZales
-Like my Facebook page:
https://www.facebook.com/AuthorDimaZales
-Follow me on Twitter:
https://twitter.com/AuthorDimaZales
-Follow me on Google+:
https://www.google.com/+DimaZales
-Friend or follow me on Goodreads:
https://www.goodreads.com/DimaZales

Thank you for your support! I truly appreciate it.

And now, please turn the page for sneak peeks into my other works.

EXCERPT FROM *THE SORCERY CODE*

Note: The book is currently FREE as an ebook at most retailers.

* * *

Once a respected member of the Sorcerer Council and now an outcast, Blaise has spent the last year of his life working on a special magical object. The goal is to allow anyone to do magic, not just the sorcerer elite. The outcome of his quest is unlike anything he could've ever imagined—because, instead of an object, he creates Her.

She is Gala, and she is anything but inanimate. Born

in the Spell Realm, she is beautiful and highly intelligent—and nobody knows what she's capable of. She will do anything to experience the world . . . even leave the man she is beginning to fall for.

Augusta, a powerful sorceress and Blaise's former fiancée, sees Blaise's deed as the ultimate hubris and Gala as an abomination that must be destroyed. In her quest to save the human race, Augusta will forge new alliances, becoming tangled in a web of intrigue that stretches further than any of them suspect. She may even have to turn to her new lover Barson, a ruthless warrior who might have an agenda of his own . . .

* * *

There was a naked woman on the floor of Blaise's study.

A beautiful naked woman.

Stunned, Blaise stared at the gorgeous creature who just appeared out of thin air. She was looking around with a bewildered expression on her face, apparently as shocked to be there as he was to be seeing her. Her wavy blond hair streamed down her back, partially covering a body that appeared to be perfection itself. Blaise tried not to think about that body and to focus on the situation instead.

A woman. A *She*, not an *It*. Blaise could hardly believe it. Could it be? Could this girl be the object?

She was sitting with her legs folded underneath her, propping herself up with one slim arm. There was something awkward about that pose, as though she didn't know what to do with her own limbs. In general, despite the curves that marked her a fully grown woman, there was a child-like innocence in the way she sat there, completely unselfconscious and totally unaware of her own appeal.

Clearing his throat, Blaise tried to think of what to say. In his wildest dreams, he couldn't have imagined this kind of outcome to the project that had consumed his entire life for the past several months.

Hearing the sound, she turned her head to look at him, and Blaise found himself staring into a pair of unusually clear blue eyes.

She blinked, then cocked her head to the side, studying him with visible curiosity. Blaise wondered what she was seeing. He hadn't seen the light of day in weeks, and he wouldn't be surprised if he looked like a mad sorcerer at this point. There was probably a week's worth of stubble covering his face, and he knew his dark hair was unbrushed and sticking out in every direction. If he'd known he would be facing a beautiful woman today, he would've done a grooming spell in the morning.

"Who am I?" she asked, startling Blaise. Her voice was soft and feminine, as alluring as the rest of her. "What is this place?"

"You don't know?" Blaise was glad he finally managed to string together a semi-coherent sentence. "You don't know who you are or where you are?"

She shook her head. "No."

Blaise swallowed. "I see."

"What am I?" she asked again, staring at him with those incredible eyes.

"Well," Blaise said slowly, "if you're not some cruel prankster or a figment of my imagination, then it's somewhat difficult to explain . . ."

She was watching his mouth as he spoke, and when he stopped, she looked up again, meeting his gaze. "It's strange," she said, "hearing words this way. These are the first real words I've heard."

Blaise felt a chill go down his spine. Getting up from his chair, he began to pace, trying to keep his eyes off her nude body. He had been expecting something to appear. A magical object, a thing. He just hadn't known what form that thing would take. A mirror, perhaps, or a lamp. Maybe even something as unusual as the Life Capture Sphere that sat on his desk like a large round diamond.

But a person? A female person at that?

To be fair, he had been trying to make the object intelligent, to ensure it would have the ability to comprehend human language and convert it into the code. Maybe he shouldn't be so surprised that the intelligence he invoked took on a human shape.

A beautiful, feminine, sensual shape.

Focus, Blaise, focus.

"Why are you walking like that?" She slowly got to her feet, her movements uncertain and strangely clumsy. "Should I be walking too? Is that how people talk to each other?"

Blaise stopped in front of her, doing his best to keep his eyes above her neck. "I'm sorry. I'm not accustomed to naked women in my study."

She ran her hands down her body, as though trying to feel it for the first time. Whatever her intent, Blaise found the gesture extremely erotic.

"Is something wrong with the way I look?" she asked. It was such a typical feminine concern that Blaise had to stifle a smile.

"Quite the opposite," he assured her. "You look unimaginably good." So good, in fact, that he was having trouble concentrating on anything but her delicate curves. She was of medium height, and so perfectly proportioned that she could've been used as a sculptor's template.

"Why do I look this way?" A small frown creased her smooth forehead. "What am I?" That last part seemed to be puzzling her the most.

Blaise took a deep breath, trying to calm his racing pulse. "I think I can try to venture a guess, but before I do, I want to give you some clothing. Please wait here—I'll be right back."

And without waiting for her answer, he hurried out of the room.

* * *

The Sorcery Code is currently FREE as an ebook at most retailers. If you'd like to learn more, please visit my website at www.dimazales.com. You can also connect with me on Facebook, Twitter, and Goodreads.

EXCERPT FROM *CLOSE LIAISONS*
BY ANNA ZAIRES

Note: *Close Liaisons* is Dima Zales's collaboration with Anna Zaires and is the first book in the internationally bestselling erotic sci-fi romance series, the Krinar Chronicles. It contains explicit sexual content and is not intended for readers under eighteen. It's also available for FREE as an ebook at most retailers.

* * *

A dark and edgy romance that will appeal to fans of erotic and turbulent relationships . . .

In the near future, the Krinar rule the Earth. An advanced race from another galaxy, they are still a mystery to us—and we are completely at their mercy.

Shy and innocent, Mia Stalis is a college student in New York City who has led a very normal life. Like most people, she's never had any interactions with the invaders—until one fateful day in the park changes everything. Having caught Korum's eye, she must now contend with a powerful, dangerously seductive Krinar who wants to possess her and will stop at nothing to make her his own.

How far would you go to regain your freedom? How much would you sacrifice to help your people? What choice will you make when you begin to fall for your enemy?

* * *

The air was crisp and clear as Mia walked briskly down a winding path in Central Park. Signs of spring were everywhere, from tiny buds on still-bare trees to the proliferation of nannies out to enjoy the first warm day with their rambunctious charges.

It was strange how much everything had changed

in the last few years, and yet how much remained the same. If anyone had asked Mia ten years ago how she thought life might be after an alien invasion, this would have been nowhere near her imaginings. *Independence Day, The War of the Worlds*—none of these were even close to the reality of encountering a more advanced civilization. There had been no fight, no resistance of any kind on government level— because *they* had not allowed it. In hindsight, it was clear how silly those movies had been. Nuclear weapons, satellites, fighter jets—these were little more than rocks and sticks to an ancient civilization that could cross the universe faster than the speed of light.

Spotting an empty bench near the lake, Mia gratefully headed for it, her shoulders feeling the strain of the backpack filled with her chunky twelve-year-old laptop and old-fashioned paper books. At twenty-one, she sometimes felt old, out of step with the fast-paced new world of razor-slim tablets and cell phones embedded in wristwatches. The pace of technological progress had not slowed since K-Day; if anything, many of the new gadgets had been influenced by what the Krinar had. Not that the Ks had shared any of their precious technology; as far as they were concerned, their little experiment had to continue uninterrupted.

Unzipping her bag, Mia took out her old Mac. The thing was heavy and slow, but it worked—and as a starving college student, Mia could not afford anything better. Logging on, she opened a blank Word document and prepared to start the torturous process of writing her Sociology paper.

Ten minutes and exactly zero words later, she stopped. Who was she kidding? If she really wanted to write the damn thing, she would've never come to the park. As tempting as it was to pretend that she could enjoy the fresh air and be productive at the same time, those two had never been compatible in her experience. A musty old library was a much better setting for anything requiring that kind of brainpower exertion.

Mentally kicking herself for her own laziness, Mia let out a sigh and started looking around instead. People-watching in New York never failed to amuse her.

The tableau was a familiar one, with the requisite homeless person occupying a nearby bench—thank God it wasn't the closest one to her, since he looked like he might smell very ripe—and two nannies chatting with each other in Spanish as they pushed their Bugaboos at a leisurely pace. A girl jogged on a path a little further ahead, her bright pink Reeboks contrasting nicely with her blue leggings. Mia's gaze followed the jogger as she rounded the corner, envying her athleticism. Her own hectic schedule allowed her little time to exercise, and she doubted she could keep up with the girl for even a mile at this point.

To the right, she could see the Bow Bridge over the lake. A man was leaning on the railing, looking out over the water. His face was turned away from Mia, so she could only see part of his profile. Nevertheless, something about him caught her attention.

She wasn't sure what it was. He was definitely tall and seemed well-built under the expensive-looking trench coat he was wearing, but that was only part of the story. Tall, good-looking men were common in model-infested New York City. No, it was something else. Perhaps it was the way he stood—very still, with no extra movements. His hair was dark and glossy under the bright afternoon sun, just long enough in the front to move slightly in the warm spring breeze.

He also stood alone.

That's it, Mia realized. The normally popular and picturesque bridge was completely deserted, except for the man who was standing on it. Everyone appeared to be giving it a wide berth for some unknown reason. In fact, with the exception of herself and her potentially aromatic homeless neighbor, the entire row of benches in the highly desirable waterfront location was empty.

As though sensing her gaze on him, the object of her attention slowly turned his head and looked directly at Mia. Before her conscious brain could even make the connection, she felt her blood turn to ice, leaving her paralyzed in place and helpless to do anything but stare at the predator who now seemed to be examining her with interest.

* * *

Breathe, Mia, breathe. Somewhere in the back of her mind, a small rational voice kept repeating those words. That same oddly objective part of her noted his symmetric face structure, with golden skin stretched tightly over high cheekbones and a firm jaw. Pictures and videos of Ks that she'd seen had hardly done them justice. Standing no more than thirty feet away, the creature was simply stunning.

As she continued staring at him, still frozen in place, he straightened and began walking toward her. Or rather stalking toward her, she thought stupidly, as his every movement reminded her of a jungle cat sinuously approaching a gazelle. All the while, his eyes never left hers. As he approached, she could make out individual yellow flecks in his light golden eyes and the thick long lashes surrounding them.

She watched in horrified disbelief as he sat down on her bench, less than two feet away from her, and smiled, showing white even teeth. No fangs, she noted with some functioning part of her brain. Not even a hint of them. That used to be another myth about them, like their supposed abhorrence of the sun.

"What's your name?" The creature practically purred the question at her. His voice was low and smooth, completely unaccented. His nostrils flared slightly, as though inhaling her scent.

"Um . . ." Mia swallowed nervously. "M-Mia."

"Mia," he repeated slowly, seemingly savoring her name. "Mia what?"

"Mia Stalis." Oh crap, why did he want to know her name? Why was he here, talking to her? In general, what was he doing in Central Park, so far away from any of the K Centers? *Breathe, Mia, breathe.*

"Relax, Mia Stalis." His smile got wider, exposing a dimple in his left cheek. A dimple? Ks had dimples? "Have you never encountered one of us before?"

"No, I haven't," Mia exhaled sharply, realizing that she was holding her breath. She was proud that her voice didn't sound as shaky as she felt. Should she ask? Did she want to know?

She gathered her courage. "What, um—" Another swallow. "What do you want from me?"

"For now, conversation." He looked like he was about to laugh at her, those gold eyes crinkling slightly at the corners.

Strangely, that pissed her off enough to take the edge off her fear. If there was anything Mia hated, it was being laughed at. With her short, skinny stature and a general lack of social skills that came from an awkward teenage phase involving every girl's nightmare of braces, frizzy hair, and glasses, Mia had more than enough experience being the butt of someone's joke.

She lifted her chin belligerently. "Okay, then, what is *your* name?"

"It's Korum."

"Just Korum?"

"We don't really have last names, not the way you do. My full name is much longer, but you wouldn't be able to pronounce it if I told you."

Okay, that was interesting. She now remembered reading something like that in *The New York Times*. So far, so good. Her legs had nearly stopped shaking, and her breathing was returning to normal. Maybe, just maybe, she would get out of this alive. This conversation business seemed safe enough, although the way he kept staring at her with those unblinking yellowish eyes was unnerving. She decided to keep him talking.

"What are you doing here, Korum?"

"I just told you, making conversation with you, Mia." His voice again held a hint of laughter.

Frustrated, Mia blew out her breath. "I meant, what are you doing here in Central Park? In New York City in general?"

He smiled again, cocking his head slightly to the side. "Maybe I'm hoping to meet a pretty curly-haired girl."

Okay, enough was enough. He was clearly toying with her. Now that she could think a little again, she realized that they were in the middle of Central Park, in full view of about a gazillion spectators. She surreptitiously glanced around to confirm that. Yep, sure enough, although people were obviously steering clear of her bench and its otherworldly occupant, there were a number of brave souls staring their way from further up the path. A couple were even cautiously filming them with their wristwatch cameras. If the K tried anything with her, it would be on YouTube in the blink of an eye, and he had to know it. Of course, he may or may not care about that.

Still, going on the assumption that since she'd never come across any videos of K assaults on college students in the middle of Central Park, she was relatively safe, Mia cautiously reached for her laptop and lifted it to stuff it back into her backpack.

"Let me help you with that, Mia—"

And before she could blink, she felt him take her heavy laptop from her suddenly boneless fingers, gently brushing against her knuckles in the process. A sensation similar to a mild electric shock shot through Mia at his touch, leaving her nerve endings tingling in its wake.

Reaching for her backpack, he carefully put away the laptop in a smooth, sinuous motion. "There you go, all better now."

Oh God, he had touched her. Maybe her theory about the safety of public locations was bogus. She felt her breathing speeding up again, and her heart rate was probably well into the anaerobic zone at this point.

"I have to go now . . . Bye!"

How she managed to squeeze out those words without hyperventilating, she would never know. Grabbing the strap of the backpack he'd just put down, she jumped to her feet, noting somewhere in the back of her mind that her earlier paralysis seemed to be gone.

"Bye, Mia. I will see you later." His softly mocking voice carried in the clear spring air as she took off, nearly running in her haste to get away.

* * *

If you'd like to find out more, please visit Anna's website at www.annazaires.com. *Close Liaisons* is currently available for FREE as an ebook at most retailers.

ABOUT THE AUTHOR

Dima Zales is a *USA Today* bestselling science fiction and fantasy author residing in Palm Coast, Florida. Prior to becoming a writer, he worked in the software development industry in New York as both a programmer and an executive. From high-frequency trading software for big banks to mobile apps for popular magazines, Dima has done it all. In 2013, he left the software industry in order to concentrate on his writing career.

Dima holds a Master's degree in Computer Science from NYU and a dual undergraduate degree in Computer Science / Psychology from Brooklyn College. He also has a number of hobbies and interests, the most unusual of which might be professional-level mentalism. He simulates mind reading on stage and close-up, and has done shows for corporations, wealthy individuals, and friends.

He is also into healthy eating and fitness, so he should live long enough to finish all the book projects he starts. In fact, he very much hopes to catch the technological advancements that might let him live forever (biologically or otherwise). Aside from that, he also enjoys learning about current and future technologies that might enhance our lives, including artificial intelligence, biofeedback, brain-to-computer interfaces, and brain-enhancing implants.

In addition to writing *The Sorcery Code* series and *Mind Dimensions* series, Dima has collaborated on a number of romance novels with his wife, Anna Zaires. The Krinar Chronicles, an erotic science fiction series, is an international bestseller and has been recognized by the likes of *Marie Claire* and *Woman's Day*. If you like erotic romance with a unique plot, please feel free to check it out, especially since the first book in the series (*Close Liaisons*) is available for free everywhere. Keep in mind, though, Anna Zaires's books are going to be much more explicit.

Anna Zaires is the love of his life and a huge inspiration in every aspect of his writing. She definitely adds her magic touch to anything Dima creates, and the books would not be the same without her. Dima's fans are strongly encouraged to learn more about Anna and her work at http://www.annazaires.com.

Made in the USA
San Bernardino, CA
10 June 2016